To Bob
Enjoy

THE TOWER HOUSE

DAVID HAY

Ashgrove fiction

First published 2011 by Ashgrove House Publishing Ltd.

Paperback ISBN 978-1-908268-15-0

Printed and bound by CPI Group (UK) Ltd, Croydon, CRO 4YY

PROLOGUE

Can you see how I live now? My twilight years.

I remember the day I bought this laptop, a week after Eva's funeral. I brought it here with me because somehow it seems to hold the key to my sanity, what's left of it.

While the other folk are having their post-lunch siesta in the lounge, or having their hair done, or their nails polished, or sitting aimlessly under the parasol in the garden, here I am tip-tapping away on my little keyboard waiting for words of comfort and release to appear as if by magic in Times bloody Roman italic on the screen.

The little Malaysian girl will be here in a minute. I know she waits for this quiet time because she's been doing it for the last month. In and out. Fussing. She wants to see what I'm writing. Help her with her 'Ingleesh'. Sometimes, I can sense her hovering outside the door when it's quiet, no alarms buzzing or lights flashing in the corridor. Mine must be the easiest room in the place to clean. No wheelchair to negotiate. No lost dentures. No pee on the toilet floor. No soiled bed.

She only knows one routine:

'Hello Thomas, how are we today?' 'Cup of tea?' ' Why are you stuck in your room on a nice day like this?' 'Shall we walk in the garden?'

Suppose I must have looked bloody odd squinting at the screen with my face all screwed up. I can still sense her tiny fingers on my hair, sliding slowly down to my ears, then removing my glasses from the top of my head and offering them to me. 'Forgot your spectacles again, Thomas.'

Only my mother called me Thomas. Still, that's the name that appears on the little card on my door, so that's who I am in here. Stops me forgetting.

Dementia. Short term memory loss. Oh yes, I have all the trappings. But I have my laptop and I must press on. I must try to complete it before it disappears like all the rest. Before it, they, you all fly away. I couldn't stop now even if I wanted to. The struggle for a reason to remember is over. The words come tumbling out, juggling for position behind the cursor. Press ENTER. That's it. I'm back. Top of the page again.

Chapter One 'My father's temper was like the wind, ...'

She's here, hovering again. I don't care. Now I know I'll finish it.

For him.

For them.

For me. For you.

1   Middlesbrough, Spring 2005

Henry Cartner suddenly noticed that he had sat behind the wheel of his car for so long that the entire windscreen had steamed up. He bunched the fingers and thumb of his right hand and gently described a small circle, directly in the line of his vacant stare, on the cold surface of misted glass. Slowly, the circle grew until a familiar line of plain white characters against a green background, brought his eyes to a focus.

TEESSIDE CHILD AND ADOLESCENCE MENTAL HEALTH SERVICE

A small red Vauxhall was the only other vehicle in the car park as he reached over to the back seat and hauled his raincoat into the front before grasping the worn and faded handle of his briefcase which had occupied the passenger seat. He stepped out into the damp morning air and, with one hand, draped the rain coat over his head and shoulders like a shawl, and locked the car.

Henry could not decide whether it was instinct or habit which prompted him to duck needlessly, every morning, as he entered the red brick Victorian house.

Casting a muted 'Morning Julie' to the receptionist who, he had often observed, wore rings on her thumbs as well as her fingers, he made his way past the bright blue plastic boxes of Lego bricks stacked neatly against the Wendy House, down a short corridor to his office.

Once inside, he flicked the light switch and inhaled deeply the familiar smells of dusty blinds, fading carpet, and damp clothes before shuffling over to his desk upon which he dropped the briefcase. Henry threw his raincoat onto a chair, took off his tweed jacket and draped it over his own seat and unclipped the brass fastener of the

briefcase. His large fingers delved inside and first removed a spectacle case, then a buff coloured file which he placed, with slow deliberation, unopened, on the pine surface of the desk. Then he sat down, closed his eyes, and contemplated the meaning of madness.

Henry had spent the majority of his adult life being certain of the uncertain, convinced of the truth of concepts and ideas which would always, it seemed to him on this grey morning, remain beyond his capability to demonstrate convincingly to others.

He had committed his life to treating many unfortunate folk who had slipped into the land of craziness as easily as they might have switched on a television set. On the other hand, he could recall the names of others who had spent months and years living out the role of dismissible and harmless eccentrics before the undeniable truth of their madness was finally recognised by colleagues, friends and family.

A couple of slow minutes passed before Henry allowed his eyes to open and his gaze to fall on the buff coloured file of Daniel Latimer. He put on his spectacles and opened it.

It was curiosity, not perplexity, which created the deep furrows on his brow as he scanned the report of his CPN, John Stockley, for the second time that morning. On the face of it, this was a fairly routine case. Typical of many. The report was written with the familiar terminology and format which he had ordered his Department to adopt. True, the language and grammar were a little clumsy in places but this was, after all, a medical statement not a bloody piece of prose.

Something exceptional has happened to this child who, to all external appearances, seemed to be a perfectly healthy ten year old of above average intelligence. Instinct told him so. Despite his problems, this boy is at ease with himself. Perhaps, too much at ease?

Henry reminded himself that many children develop imaginary friends who are subsequently discarded, simply grown out of, without any lasting harm; while other kids often display symptoms of sullen, adolescent moodiness and isolation at a depressingly early age.

The behaviour which Daniel was demonstrating was not typical of his peers but was, by no stretch of the imagination, unusual. So why had this case been hastily referred to him?

Daniel, what has happened here?

He picked up the telephone,

'John, g'morning. How was the parents evening last night?'

He waited patiently while the CPN recounted his discussions with the teachers of his eldest child.

'So you wouldn't get back in time for the first half of the match then… ah well…great goal.'

Henry found it useful to feign an interest in football, if it meant that he could quickly establish rapport with colleagues.

'Listen, .John, I wonder if you wouldn't mind popping down for a few minutes to go over the Daniel Latimer case. I'm seeing the boy's mum later on this morning and I just want to make sure I've got the whole picture here.'

By the time John Stockley appeared at the door of his office, Henry had scanned the file and appraised himself, yet again, of the basic facts of the case.

Daniel, youngest son of Richard aged forty and Fiona aged thirty eight, brother of Philip aged thirteen, referred because of anxiety and behavioural difficulties over the past seven months. Introverted at home and school, he has developed a close attachment to an imaginary friend with whom he appears to share his thoughts and feelings. At school, he has become disinterested and non-communicative until challenged when he has then been disruptive in lessons to the point where his teachers have expressed concern, and he is now being teased and ostracised by other pupils. Mrs Latimer revealed a similar pattern of behaviour at home, over the last few months, with regard to spending most of his time alone in his bedroom or in the garden. Mr Latimer states that at the present time things are worse than ever, following a meeting with the school headmaster, where they are now considering Daniels future. Mrs Latimer states that Daniel has always been an outgoing and popular little boy, but they feel that as a family they are having difficulty managing his current behaviour, obviously they feel that Daniel needs some support regarding the issues at school.

Henry looked up from the notes.

'John, thanks for this. Take me through what the boy himself thinks about all this?

Not that there's anything wrong with your report. I just want to hear it from you.'

'Well, basically, Daniel believes it is other people who are having difficulties and not him, and he doesn't understand why there is a fuss or why he has been brought here. He reports difficulty concentrating when people start losing their temper with him and when other children start calling him names but the rest of the time he is happy. Obviously, his words not mine.'

'Go on, please,' urged Henry.

'At school, he gets very cross when the teachers and the other boys want him to say and do things all the time because often he just wants to think and be quiet with his new friend. He tells me that the situation is just the same at home and that he doesn't think he wants any help but he would like someone to tell him why everybody is miserable with him. I think this is an area where he would like some help.'

'Tell me about the family. How does he get on with them?'

'Apart from Mum, Dad and brother Philip, there's little extended family, so Daniel has no close contacts outside of them. He told me that he thinks he has a good relationship with his dad but it used to be better, and he did actually admit that he had been spoilt in the past. But now he reckons Richard likes Philip better, and that his dad is always so busy at work that they don't spend much time together.77 He sometimes doesn't see him during the week when he is at school a lot but, at the weekends, dad tries to spend time with him. He describes his dad as getting cross very easily, and bossy, wanting him to do things that he used to enjoy but now finds boring.'

Henry raised a hand, 'His dad, Richard, is a self employed architect... right?'

John nodded 'Correct. Pretty successful I think.'

'How does he get on with Mum?'

'Daniel told me his relationship with his mum is good but he also said that in the last few weeks she has been getting easily stressed, and gets cross and miserable. He says that, most of the time, both parents are OK with him and they try to talk to him but they don't seem to understand that ....his words again.....he likes to be on his own and with his friend. That's when there are lots of rows.'

'I see' Henry muttered to himself, 'Go on please. What about the brother?'

'Well, it seems that he used to play a lot with his brother Philip and try to beat him at games which he sometimes won, and they sometimes used to fight. But they don't do anything like that any more. Daniel did say that his brother doesn't talk to him very much but he's not really bothered about that. He described his parents relationship as a good one but I felt that he was holding something back on that one. I didn't press him on it. The boy clearly believes that Richard favours his brother over him but he also feels that he himself is his mums favourite. He reckons his parents say nasty and horrible things to him at times, when they are particularly cross at his behaviour, but they don't smack him or hit him or anything like that.'

John paused as the telephone rang.

When Henry had dealt with the call, he announced 'Mrs Latimer has arrived.'

The CPN rose from his chair.

'No no. Just a minute John. I want a little more. What do the parents themselves think?'

'Well...er....she told me that she feels that family relationships are okay but is aware that the close bond between Daniel and Philip has disappeared.

When I spoke to Mr Latimer, he did admit to sometimes making aggressive comments to Daniel and at times praising Philip in order to push Daniel a bit harder. Mrs Latimer did allude to the fact that at times she feels she is being a bad mother and did appear to be able to understand how the family's relationships may have impacted on Daniel.'

'And Philip, the brother?'

'Philip describes his younger brother as a wally and clearly is embarrassed by what he sees as his kid brother's strange behaviour at school.'

Henry glanced again at the file. No problems with Daniel's birth. Either pre or post- natal. All developmental milestones reached appropriately. Described as a young child who had always been fidgety, outgoing and impulsive. First childhood memory is of a family holiday in France. Not many clues here. No signs of self harm. Says he is happiest when he is on his own and with his new best friend. Does not give a name for his friend. Remains silent when pressed to do so. No evidence of formal depressive illness. His major wishes are to be left alone and that everyone will stop fussing.

'Thanks John. I appreciate your time. I'd better not keep Mrs Latimer waiting any longer.'

Fiona Latimer knew precisely what she needed and wanted from the appointment.

A label. A label to describe Daniels condition. Something to make people take her seriously. To describe the anxiety and sheer bewilderment which was dominating her life.

She reminded herself that Daniel was a bright ten year old. Intelligent, gifted even, from a safe and comfortable home, in Little Smeaton for Heavens sake. He was loved.

How she longed for a clear diagnosis with a proper name so that she and Richard could refute any suggestion that their younger son had learning difficulties. A label, a name to give to this distressing condition which had turned her happy little boy into a withdrawn and

sensitive recluse. A signpost which would quickly open the door to help and treatment: counselling or private tuition maybe, some books to study, or even a change of diet, some exercises or medicine.

Her eyes never strayed for a second from the large crumpled man before her, half rimmed spectacles perched midway along his meandering nose. A bright red handkerchief flopped lazily out of the breast pocket of his brown jacket and clashed badly, she observed, with the pale blue bow tie squashed under dark jowls as his heavy face sagged down towards the papers cradled in his lap.

Henry glanced down at the floor, removed his spectacles and reflected on the report.

'You live at Little Smeaton, Mrs Latimer. Lovely spot.'

'Daniel thinks it terribly boring, I'm afraid.'

'He goes to Prep School.'

'Yes. He'll follow Philip to the grammar. We're very fortunate to be able to send the boys to good schools. I'm afraid they both get pretty much everything they need..£20 per week pocket money. Until all this happened, we were....oh I don't know...blissful I suppose...if that's not too smug.'

'Not at all' replied Henry.

'Until Daniel started to become...the way he is....he seemed so...alive. Now he spends his time in his room. Perfectly happy on his own. That's hard enough but the school situation. And this friend of his. The one who has no name. The invisible one. No wonder the other kids at school pick on him.'

'Are you angry with him, Mrs Latimer?'

She flushed 'Don't be silly...Daniel's my son. I adore him.'

'You're allowed to be angry,' he smiled.

' Doctor Carter...It's so....I'm just so worried about him..'

'It's Cartner actually, Mrs Latimer' he smiled, immediately regretting the remark,

He still held the report in his large hands. Why were these moments still so difficult for him after all these years? Trying to put people at ease, but wanting to be accurate, logical. Somehow, the two things seemed to be difficult to reconcile.

2   Billingham, Spring 1927

My father's temper was like the wind and I have always been aware that I take after him. There is a mischievous breeze that often plays across the broad plain of the Tees Valley, coming in eastwards from the high Pennines in the west, skirting round the Cleveland Hills and the foothills of the North Yorkshire Moors on its way towards the grey North Sea. It flatters to deceive, rarely threatens, and is largely ignored by the men and women who live here. Then it can turn north easterly with real menace, shifting huge clouds and rearranging the sky in a few minutes. In winter, such Arctic gusts are always harshest close to the Tees itself, and it is only then that the people bend to the elements, waiting for the raw sting in the air to be replaced by the pale, quiet stillness, after the wind has passed on to leave a promise of warm summer days to be nurtured and remembered.

Matthew Devlin's anger never erupted into violence, and in many ways brought our house to life and instilled in me an early sense of expressive freedom, which I still take for granted. To me, our father's rages were a perfectly acceptable trade- off in return for his open, honest nature. If it was in him, sooner or later it would come out. My brother and I could always tell his mood from the way he held his pipe: two fingers over the top of the stem with the thumb underneath meant that he was figuring something out and would not take kindly to an interruption, pointing downwards meant he was relaxed and amenable, thumb and fingers concealing the barrel meant watch out and, if the thumb was tapping the side of the barrel, then a hurricane was brewing. He was not yet forty but looked older, with greying curly hair, lined, shrewd eyes and the belligerent ruddy countenance of his Irish forebears, the years of hard toil in the shipyards of Haverton Hill having taken their toll on his heavy frame.

Though there was little to spare, we never knew hardship

My mother Agnes adored her Matty, and hers was the only face to which he readily submitted, so that was how my parents world worked, the two of them bound together by the very polarity of their natures. Where my brother Bill and I were concerned, she conceded all aspects of discipline to Matty, and all praise and all punishment likewise, but the standards to which we were expected to adhere were undoubtedly hers. We regarded the regular frog-march to church in our Sunday togs as a cruel punishment to be avoided if possible, while she, steeped in the ways of the Church of England, took pride, solace and comfort from it. She would stand us in the back room kitchen for inspection, nod in the direction of the passage to the vestibule where we would wait on the blue and red tiled floor, gather herself together, and sweep past us, out through the big front door, down the steps between the painted green railings which enclosed our raised garden beneath the bay window, to lead from the front. Our father preferred the comfort of his bed on Sunday mornings, having long ago abandoned the "One True Faith" of his Irish heritage. Born of agricultural stock, her roots were in the soil from which our village was born, while Matty's family had been migrants seeking labour and a new life in the industrial north, but she had always known that he was much more than a ships plater.

Further away from the river, the wind is often kinder, leaving the tributaries more protected and attractive to migratory birds and other wildlife.

In that March of 1927, the gales were replaced by a brief respite of clinging, mild, damp air under thin clouds, with only a light breeze to gently shift the trees and hedgerows. By May, each dawn saw the sun flare down, burning off the dampness, making the short grass sing and creating a soft heat haze well before mid morning. From its high vantage point overlooking the beck valley we called "The Bottoms", the old Saxon tower of Saint Cuthbert's stood guard over Billingham, as it had for the past dozen centuries. Our church school was the centrepiece of the green, built in 1852, its five classrooms and two tiny yards at either end over-spilling with a new generation of post war children and the offspring of the incomer worker families. Directly in front of it stood the village cross, made of Shap granite, imposing atop its four wide steps, and around it were the cottages and terraced houses, Charlie Pool's garage, Fletcher's grocery shop, the cobblers, a few shops, the inns, farm houses and outbuildings, that huddled around the edge of the green. At the eastern end of the green, a tall chimney dominated the view, part of a small brewery owned by the Heslop Company and directly behind a grander row of properties which included the School House, an elegant eighteenth century manor house once occupied by the brewery owner, and a large Georgian house adjacent Lower Grange Farm.

The hand painted sign outside Charlie Pool's place offered complete overhauls, brazing, spares, tyres and carbide, and was a magnet for small boys who were drawn by its heady mixture of petrol fumes, engine noises, oily rags, polish and chrome among the line up of motorbikes, side-cars and bicycles which stood proudly on parade at the front of his place. At ten each morning, his converted Morris Cowley van would make its morning run to collect parcels from the railway station and bring them back to the village with a large sheet for receipt signatures. To the side of the shop front, next

11

to another smaller sign which said 'Agent for BSA and Royal Ruby Cycles', the 'Pinnacle' stood four storeys tall in smartly dressed white brick, one small room on top of another and then another as if in defiant challenge of its near neighbour, the church tower. No one quite knew how it grew to be so tall, but the story went that George 'Taty' Robson, a renowned potato grower, blacksmith, grocer and all round local entrepreneur had been denied permission to expand his building site and so decided to build upwards instead. The folly we called the 'Pinnacle' turned out to be his lasting legacy to our village, and never failed to instil a sense of fascination and curiosity in me.

Just behind the green to the south was our terraced house in South View, and across the road, the new houses built by Nesco, the electric company. Long established farms and smallholdings were to the north, either side of the embankment carrying the Clarence railway from Stockton to Hartlepool, forking just beyond the station where the track branched off to reach the new shipyards and factories around the north bank of the river, where the relentless spread of industry was transforming the landscape. To the west, the 'staff houses', a row of elegant, white, detached properties had appeared on the bank leading down to the Bottoms, built for those who ran the Synthetic, as we still called the new chemical company.

Jesse Coupar was not a clever boy, but this seldom occurred to those who were easily impressed by his persuasive way with simple words, as were my brother Bill and I. There were too many dropped aitches and harsh vowel sounds rattling off his tongue to render him well-spoken in the social sense; but it was, nevertheless, a compelling voice. No physical feature distinguished him in any noticeable way from the rest of the lads, but the steady gaze which shone from those clear blue eyes never failed to add a peculiar intensity and weight to the words of one so young.

The Coupar family were from the land: labourers who, for the past few generations at least, had kept the wolves from their door by taking whatever work was available from the farms and smallholdings of South Durham. In recent years, they had settled in a tiny tied cottage near Wolviston, which provided some stability for their unusually small family of two sons and a daughter. Jesse was the middle child and had grown up straight and strong, with few of the childhood illnesses which beleaguered the growth of his siblings. He found his comforts in the friendships forged among the children of the local villages, particularly Billingham where he attended our school.

Bill and I never got to see Jesse's home, and we maintained a silent respect for his right to keep his own counsel on family matters. Somehow, it didn't seem to matter to us. Jesse was just Jesse. A will o' the wisp who would turn up at unexpected times and then disappear just as quickly as he had arrived.

We should not have been at the Bottoms that morning. Jesse and our Bill were lying face down near the edge of the beck, with me in between them, almost motionless, the backs of our legs stinging under the beating sun. Once again, slowly, Bill wriggled forward on his stomach and stretched out his arm towards the water, in his grip a twisted branch from which a jam jar was suspended by a short length of string. As we looked on, he lowered the jar into the beck and waited. Silent minutes passed before the jam jar was hoisted from the water and held aloft to the sun.

I remember pleading 'Hold it still, here let me see, you're holding it too high.'

For the sixth time that morning, my elder brother placed the jar gently into my eager hands and I held it against my nose to peer through the glass.

'Still can't see no sticklebacks'

Bill slowly folded his arms, bent his knees to lower himself until his eyes were level with the jar and carefully examined it again and again, rubbing his eyes slowly and sadly before he was compelled to agree.

'You said we'd get loads and we haven't and we better soon ad or we're right in it and you said. You did.....you did our Bill.'

It was an unspoken understanding in our sibling relationship that such pressure would inevitably yield some sort of dividend, but this time Bill simply retrieved the jar from my grasp, gave a long sigh, and slowly poured the green contents on to the ground.

'Stop yer whining Tommy man, it'll be alright,' was all I was offered.

I kicked his shin, but he barely flinched, 'Oh sure, and what do we say to Miss Bateman? How we gonna sneak back in to school? What if she gets us up in front of old Raper? You said we'd catch loads and loads and then we'd be back before they saw us gone. You said Bill.'

This time, there was no response at all. There was an awful silence. My throat began to tighten with an anxious sense of foreboding, the warm sun now attacking the back of my neck and ears, already pulsing to the thumping rhythm coming from deep in my chest. I thought I caught a glimpse of fear in Bill's face, as hesitation seemed to paralyse us. Then the moment was gone.

'Try over there.'

Our heads turned towards the voice.

Jesse had remained motionless, still lying on his front at the very edge of the beck, staring out across its surface. I waited for Bill to say something but he seemed to just hover there at my side, his right hand clutching the twisted branch, gently swinging it and causing the jar to sway to and fro, catching intense flashes of sunlight.

Jesse broke the silence once more.

'Over there by them reeds, that's where they are.'

We went for it.

My recollection of everything that happened next has crystallised over the years into a multi-faceted crystal, a gallery of familiar images which I can conjure up at will, each diamond sharp and etched deep in my memory. Ripples in the sparkling beck as the jar disappeared among the reeds. A pair of long tailed tits. Tiny droplets of water catching the sunlight, cascading from the jar and sprinkling carelessly on our upturned faces as we held the twisted branch aloft. Then suddenly a shoal of sticklebacks circling the glass jar, magnified. Bill and I bouncing and yelling. Jesse's freckles dark on his nose, teeth gleaming in that wide, triumphal grin. The three of us taking turns to bear our quarry back along the track to the footpath, floating on a cushion of joy towards the climbing road that would carry us up to the green and our school.

It was then, a short way up Billingham Bank road, that we paused for a breather and to take another opportunity to inspect the sticklebacks. Bill bent forward to support himself, his hands on his bare knees, face to the pavement. I copied him, and felt under my sweating palms the pieces of pressed, damp grass that were still clinging there.

'So what are we gonna say' I managed.

'You think of something.'

'Like what?'

'I dunno, think of something. Maybe if we wait till the dinner break we can just walk straight in there an' nobody will be any the wiser.'

Indignant, I aimed a kick at his legs but in truth it was a half-hearted effort 'Yeah, and maybe they will.'

'Let me think,' Bill was never shy of pondering solutions in public.

There was nothing I could do but ponder along beside him, picturing our inevitable fate in a tableau of scenes that tumbled around in my fevered imagination: a humiliating lecture in front of the class, standing in the corner all afternoon, hauled in front of the whole school, maybe the ruler, the slipper, the cane, banishment for a week, sent away somewhere, never seeing my friends again, ever, and worse.....the look of shame in my mothers eyes, abandoned to the wrath of my father's judgement.

As the sweat again started to form a thin film under my chin, I turned to face Jesse who was staring intently at a painted wooden sign upon which were painted the words LUMSDENS OF NEWCASTLE, MASTER BUILDERS, CONTRACTORS FOR MAIN OFFICE. He stretched, hands on his hips, to take in the avenue of young trees behind which two new, white staff houses stood in proud detachment, occasionally turning his attention to the men who were digging out foundations for more to be built further row along the road.

'Well?' I ventured.

'Well what?'

'Thought of somethin'?'

'Yes'

'Well what?'

He turned to me and smiled, then glanced back at the builders sign 'I'm wondrin' who's gonna live 'ere, and why it isn't us.'

Exasperated, I paused to search Bill's face for support. There was none.

'That's it?'

Jesse turned his face fully to mine, his faced wreathed in an open smile, 'Come on. Lets go back to school. Don't worry Tommy.'

We set off again, and I felt his hand on my shoulder.

'We'll tell old Raper that Miss Bateman's nature lesson on Monday gave us ideas an' so we couldn't wait to see for ourselves what we could get from Billy Beck an' bring it back to show 'em all what we caught. Then we'll tell 'em we can't wait for another of her lessons and how we love the nature stuff. Come on. Its gonna be alright Tommy boy.'

Rounding the corner at the top of the road by Church End Farm, we could hear the noisy activity of children as the village cross and the iron railings around the yard of our little red brick school came in to view, and I knew that I could find no reason on earth to doubt him.

3

We wouldn't do it again, that much Bill and I promised ourselves. A few pieces of Meccano lay scattered on the small, clipped mat at the foot of the double bed which occupied most of our bedroom at the back of the house, bathed now in the soft light of early evening as we reflected on the labours of the day. I went to the window and positioned two lead soldiers side by side, their bases planted firmly on cigarette cards, to guard the window sill. Outside, the low sun cast deep shadows over the back yards, giving sharp definition to everything that wasn't already shaded for the night. I rested my chin on my hands and let my eyes wander over the corrugated steel roof and the chimney from our brick copper, beside it the big wheel of the mangle with its wooden rollers, the dry closet and the steel dust bin next to it, behind which a line of string hung limply from a length of twisted branch which was propped up against the wall of the yard.

'Still, too close but,' I murmured to the window pane.

'You what?'

'Could've got in real trouble, nickin' off like that you know.'

'Well we didn't' observed Bill, as his fingers carefully manoeuvred little brass nuts and bolts, fastening them to red and green plates with fierce concentration.

'I know, but we coulda' I insisted.

'But we didn't'

'Coulda'

'Didn't'

'Coulda'

'Didn't'

I turned away from the window and crouched down next to Bill. This conversation needed to be nudged along; something was missing, something to round it all off, some sort of conclusion, something that would seal our triumph …but I couldn't find it.

I offered, 'Thanks to Jesse.'

'Yeah. Thanks to him.'

'I know.'

'I know.'

There, it had all been said, and yet still something inside me believed there was still an element of unresolved business that Bill and I had not concluded, and it refused to let me go. I watched as some little brass wheels were fastened on to spindles with tiny black retaining clips.

'Bill?'

'Hmm?'

'What Jesse said'

Bill looked up from his construction.

I ploughed on, 'Well, like. He didn't even fib did he? It just came out just like it really was. You know. Like he said. Batey's nature lesson, and the jar and them sticklebacks and all of it. You know what I mean, our Bill?'

He resumed his work with the screwdriver and tiny spanner.

'Yeah, I know.'

As the light began to fade, we heard the vestibule door close and the voice of our mother, then the front door opening and closing and our mother returning to the passage. We raced to the front of the house, to the coolness of our parents bedroom.

Below, a figure dressed in black was descending the steps to the pavement, wearing a large black hat, like a bowler from which a black veil hung down to her shoulders. I recognised her as Miss Northcote, a woman of infinite mystery who was never referred to by my mother by her first name, but always by the curious title of 'lady worker.' She stopped at the pavement as, just at that moment, my father approached on his sturdy, upright bike, his face ruddy face glowing from the exertion of his ride from the shipyard. His right leg slowly raised itself away from the pedal and up and over the cross-bar, as it had done a thousand times, and the bike was brought to a sedate halt at Miss Northcote's feet. We watched as he doffed his cap and shared a few short pleasantries before she made her way back towards the cottages at the end of our road, his eyes following her for a few yards before he wheeled his bike towards the archway which divided the second and third houses in our block of four. As he disappeared into the cut, we returned to our own bedroom in time to see him open the gate to our yard and rest his bike against the wall. As the gate swung shut behind him, the twisted branch slowly slid down the side of the wall and rested itself behind the dustbin, a small piece of the string still just visible, trailing on the floor of the yard.

'Good, that means we'll get our teas soon, now she's gone and our Dads 'ome" said Bill, as we carefully returned the Meccano to its box, and closed the lid with its picture of two boys, dressed in red and blue v- necked cardigans and straight grey socks, cross legged, their hair as shiny and combed as if it had just been Brylcreemed, in front of a roaring fire in their

17

sitting room of all places, working on a huge crane nearly as big as a bed, their father smiling approvingly from his armchair.

Soon, bolstered by a strange sense of pride, we almost marched downstairs to the back kitchen we called our living room where my mother was silhouetted against the window, her fingers nervously playing with the edge of her pinnie while my father stood stiffly in front of his chair, feet planted firmly on the mat which covered the tiles by the fireplace, tapping his pipe on the bracket swinging out above the fire, from which the kettle hung motionless. As we entered, he eased himself into the chair, the barrel of his pipe obscured by the fingers and thumb of his huge right hand.

'Well now, it's the nature boys is it?' his eyes never leaving my mothers.

Bill drew up a chair and made to sit at the small table. As I instinctively followed, we were interrupted.

'Before any food is eaten in this house tonight, I want to know what the two of you were doing, down by the Bottoms on a school morning.' The pipe was pointed at each of us in turn.

'Well, like we 'ad this lesson...on Monday it was...with Batey...' I blurted out.

'Miss Bateman to you,' the flat voice of my mother came from the window.

'And we 'ad to go.....an then...'

He rose from his seat as I continued to search for the words, the style, the look with which Jesse had delivered our tale, first to Miss Bateman, then to the Headmaster Mr Raper, then to the assembled school. His head went back, then forward, his heels lifting off the mat in a rocking motion until finally his voice exploded,

'STOP! For the love of God. Stop right there.'

A terrible silence hung in the sitting room, as I edged closer to Bill who managed to whisper quietly 'Honest to God, Dad...'

'A little less of the gods, please,' came from the window.

My father turned to her, 'Your mother and me have heard the tale, and a very fine one it is. And I suppose you were thinking that's the end of it eh? Well here's another one. Nature is it? I'll give you nature. You will go to see Miss Bateman tomorrow and you will apologise and you will tell her this. Listen mind. Tell her that the three of you will help out with Stan Smith on the digging, up by Chapel Road, and you'll be there helpin' till its all dug over...all of it ...fit for vegetables. '

I looked up into Bills face at my side, but could only see incomprehension in his eyes and so concluded, with a measure of forlorn regret, that a strategy of patience was required and a full explanation of our sentence would have to wait until later.

'Nature indeed,' exclaimed my mother, as if wanting to conclude the proceedings.

It wasn't quite over, 'And if I hear of you, either of you, missing your school again, I'll tan your backsides so I will' he boomed.

'Having to hear it from the Lady Worker,' my mother shuddered.

The room went quiet again, my mother took the kettle from the copper by the fire and went out into the yard to draw water, while my father eased himself back into his seat and placed his fingers over the stem of his pipe, his thumb supporting it from below, placing it slowly to his lips.

The sound of the kitchen clock was the only noise to accompany the preparation of our meal, but as we sat down and began to eat I rediscovered my appetite until Bill broke the ice.

'Dad, what does Mister Smith want the land dug over for at Chapel Road?'

My father slowly rested his knife and fork on the side of his place, wiped his mouth with the back of his left hand and, placing his elbows firmly on the table, was about to speak when my mother interrupted.

'Its next to where the new church school is going to be.'

'A new school for us?' Bill asked.

'For the infants, not for you, you'll stay at the Green' she explained.

'When do we get ours then' I enquired.

'Nothing wrong with your school, boy. Good enough for you. As you would know if you and your brother here condescended to go,' observed my father, resuming his meal.

'But Dad' I went on.

'Eat, Thomas' my mother's finger tapped the table.

'Let the boy have his say, Aggie. Go on then son, let's hear it'

I had a platform, now all I needed was a speech.

I coughed, wiped my mouth and carefully placed down my knife and fork, resting them on the edge of my plate, planted my elbows on the table and paused for effect.

'It's like we do a lot of waitin'.....'

My words hung in the air, hovered above the table, and disappeared into the evening. Bill seemed about to speak, hesitated, and thought better of it. It was my father who eventually began,

'Waiting?'

'Yeah. Waitin' for new lavvies. Like them over the road. And for 'lectric stead of our gas lamps. An now there's gonna be a new school 'cept we not getting one an....'

My father's hand went up, signalling an end to my speech.

'Well now. So this house no longer suits your Lordship's requirements, is that it?'

He sat back in his chair 'As it happens, there's been a letter from the council which might please you, sir, if you could understand it, sir, which you will, if you go to school, which you also will.....sir...and we're on the list.'

'There now,' my mother was smiling as she rose from her seat and reached out to begin clearing away the plates.

'But when?' I persisted.

'Soon.'

'But when though?'

'ENOUGH!'

Knives and forks bounced on the wooden surface and a teaspoon spun away in a crazy arc and fell to the tiles below as my father's clenched fist slammed down on the table, 'Does this boy not believe his father?'

My mother brushed her hands down the front of her pinnie and resumed her seat, slowly shaking her head, her hand gently resting for a second on mine as she whispered softly 'Doubting Thomas.'

Bill chipped in 'That's what Miss Bateman calls him in school.'

'So?' I retorted.

'It's from the Bible.'

'I know that.I'm not stupid, our Bill. Tell him Mam. I'm not. Every time she tells off Danny Thomas, she goes like this,' I rolled my eyes to dramatic effect and made an effort at Miss Bateman's well-modulated accent 'Into the lion's den once more Daniel.'

A flicker of a smile appeared on my mother's face.

'And then when Pete Fletcher gets 'is sums right again she says, Peter my rock. So I'm not daft, am I Mam?'

Bill grinned and punched my arm, then my mother intervened 'Your father said enough, now let that be an end and help me clear these things away.'

'Anyway,' I retaliated 'that's how I knew 'ow Jesse found them sticklebacks in Billy Beck. Cos of 'is name.'

'What are you talking about, our Tommy?'

20

'Cos Jesse must 'ave been a fisherman, like in the Bible' I went on.

My mother's confused expression was clearly noted by my father who rolled his eyes upwards to the ceiling, 'Now how the blazes did you come up with that one, I'd like to know.?'

'Cos in class,' I beamed confidently 'Miss Bateman, she said, in the Bible hymns and stuff, she said that great things came from Jesse's line.'

My mother coughed and stood bolt upright, then began methodically picking up the plates, knives, forks spoons, as much as she could gather in her hands, while my father's eyes danced with delight as he gave out a mighty roar of laughter. His hand reached over the table and ruffled my hair.

'Go help your mother now,' was all he needed to say.

4

The vicarage stood in isolated grandeur at the head of a small narrow row of low-beamed, fussy old cottages. Running behind its grounds, next to the high wall of the churchyard, was a large plot of waste ground, overgrown with grass, weeds, bushes, rocks and stones of every shape and size.

As we approached the place of punishment, I plunged my hands deep into my pockets and edgily retreated further behind Bill and Jesse until we were within twenty yards of the gate where my curiosity was aroused by the low murmur of small voices.

One hand resting on a spade, the other on his right hip, Stan Smith smiled slowly at our entrance and nodded an unspoken order to line up at the end of the row of sad, familiar, figures awaiting their fate.

'Better late than never' he observed, thrusting the spade into the earth at his feet to commence the inspection of his workforce, 'Now then, who knows how to use a spade properly?'

I took some comfort from the silence that followed.

'Nobody eh?'

He paced back and forth in front of the line up and stopped next to Joe, a pal who lived just a couple of doors away, and handed him the spade.

'Go on Joe, show me'

Joe took a determined, confident hold on the implement and searched among the long grass and weeds for a clear patch where he could make some kind of impression, eventually discovering a tiny circle of loose soil, where he planted his right foot firmly on the ground, using his left to dig in to the earth.

I was impressed.

'Alright Joe, that's a start at least. Here, give the spade to me' said Mister Smith, waving him back into the line up.

'Wrong foot. Use the right foot, like this'

We took a turn each before we were paired off to mark out a small plot of ground, me with Jesse, Bill with Guy Henderson, Joe with Bill Greenley and so on until there was a pair of partners allocated to all parts of the plot.

The work commenced in silence which soon grew to be more oppressive than the heat, as we sullenly set to our task, each boy wearing a martyred expression, bent double to pick up the loose stones first, placing them in neat piles at the edge of their patch.

'Got any water?' I asked Jesse. He looked up from the small pile of stones at his feet.

'Ave you Jesse?'

Mister Smith called out 'Two more minutes boys, then we'll break off ' A drone of approval spread through the labourers as he gingerly clambered past a couple of nettle bushes towards the far end of the churchyard wall from where he produced a small box, lifting it over his head. Inside the box were apples, and several bottles of water which we consumed in silence, taking stock of our progress as we surveyed the scene.

'Why don't we pile all of the little stones together in one ruddy great pile so it'll look bigger, like we've done loads an' loads?' whispered Bill Greenley, 'Then we can start on the biguns.'

So it was that each pair of boys added a quota of small stones until the pile grew into a sizeable heap near to the gate, and by the end of the second afternoon we had started to shift some of the larger ones. On the third evening, we kept back one of the water bottles and a couple of apples from Mister Smith's supply and sat like Red Indian braves in a circle under the shade of a large tree on the edge of the green, opposite the school.

Every afternoon of that week, we hacked away at the long grass, weeds, bushes and rubbish, slowly exposing the dry, bare earth that had remained hidden for so long, now pale and hard from the absence of rain and moisture. By Friday, it was virtually cleared and we rewarded ourselves with a visit to Picketts Pool at the Bottoms, deep and wide enough for us to dive in naked, our boots and clothes left on the banks to the mercy of a small group of Norton lads who whooped and jeered as they flung them gleefully into the air.

No matter, it was comfort not anger that we shared that evening. Comfort in being alive, in sharing the aching in our limbs, in the feel of the cold water on our bodies, in the laughter of the confusion as we fumbled around in the twilight to retrace our pants, socks and far flung shoes.

The following week, we began digging, raking and hoeing our patches of ground until the arrival of Thursday evening when Mister Smith finally announced 'Boys, I think that's it. After tomorrow, I won't be needing you any more.' He grinned at Bill and I 'You can go back to your fishing.'

As the shadow of the churchyard wall grew long, the mild evening air filled with insects and chattering birdsong, smelling of burnt, smoky grass which, somehow, seemed to lay heavily on all of us as we looked back over the flat smooth tilth of the newly tendered plot. Mister Smith gathered up the last of the water bottles and packed them away in the box as a general air of solemnity seemed to float down, silently to the earth, glowing now at our feet with a soft warmth, still bone dry but no longer wild and untamed.

23

I had imagined this moment and the eager anticipation of walking back down Chapel Lane with Bill and the others, and had turned to walk away when I felt a small object under my right foot and held on to Joe to balance myself as I dislodged a small pebble from the sole of my boot. Perfectly round and smooth, a milky white colour with ruddy brown markings as if painted by an artist with a fine brush, it seemed to burn and glow in my hand. I strode out onto the broad even earth, I tossed it into the air and, when it fell, swung out my right boot, striking it with perfect timing so that it flew towards the far wall where it disappeared into the shadows, the cracking sound making a faint echo. Then I thrust my fist into the air.

'No more blisters, c'mon lets go home.'

I knew all the boys were watching and listening, and that they heard me, but nobody spoke and not one of them was moving as they stared forlornly at the scarred earth where my boots had left their clear imprint and the deep, narrow furrow where my boot had gouged out the soil. It was as if they were all disorientated.

I shuffled back into the row of boys. Mister Smith raised his voice 'Well off yer go then lads, straight home mind.'

Still nobody moved until Joey broke ranks and took off his shirt, handed it to Guy Henderson and knelt onto the ground, smoothing it over with his bare hands, letting the earth break through his fingers time and again. Bill Greenley knelt beside Joey and together we watched them brushing the soil gently with their arms until it was flat once more.

Then Jesse strode purposefully around the edge of the newly tendered land towards the wall where we peered at him among the gloomy shadows, bending low here and there, his hand occasionally raking the ground, stroking it slowly and gently.

I called out 'What are you doin' Jesse?'

A few more seconds passed before he emerged from the shadows, smiling, his hand extended towards mine so that, instinctively, I offered him my open palm. His eyes fixed on mine for a few seconds as I fought to hold back the welling tears before I felt my hand snap shut, closing tightly like a clam, the digits folding over the pebble which he had dropped into its grasp.

24

5   Little Smeaton, Spring 2005

The west elevation of the Cedars created a flat grey monolith in the late evening mist which shrouded the house. Huddled on the broad Yorkshire stone patio stretching the breadth of the property, the outline shape of garden furniture could be made out, wrapped in dark green tarpaulined parcels on which the damp air had formed a multitude of tiny water bubbles.

On the other side of the house, a porch light flashed its security glare across the red gravel drive where a large four wheeled passenger carrier slowly circled to a halt before depositing a waving, track-suited figure at the front entrance.

Inside the Cedars, the local TV teatime news echoed around the dining kitchen.

From his vantage point at the top of the long landing above the impressive staircase, Richard Latimer gazed out over the expanse of herring bone wood flooring of the entrance hall as his first born, Phil, burst in and headed straight towards the kitchen. Below, he could hear his wife's voice above the sound of the news announcer, then the beginnings of a conversation, but the words were indistinguishable to him as his palms gripped the banister rail.

Slowly, his tight grasp relaxed with a deep sigh as he allowed himself another sideways glance along the passage of immaculate, evenly spaced maple doors. He had already paced the landing three times, and now he returned again to the third door on the left, on which he had screwed, tight jawed, a white ceramic plate bearing the message in bold red letters 'Daniels Room'. He had been unable, of course, to resist Fiona's pleading for this small concession, this tiny nod to youthful independence. Now, it almost seemed to be mocking him as his knuckles tapped gently on the panel of maple.

'Daniel ?'

There was no sound from within, as he turned the handle, opening the door sufficiently to enable him to place his head in the gap and peer inside.

'Daniel ?'

His youngest son was lying on his bed at the far side of the bedroom, his face to the ceiling, in his hands a bright red book.

'Phil's back from training, Mum's about to serve up'.

'About time, I'm starved'.

Richard felt his shoulders ease as he shuffled further into the room, hands in pocket,   stopping at the foot of the bed where he made an

25

exaggerated swivelling movement with his hips, and bent double at the waist to peer intently at the cover of Daniels book which displayed the title 'Boro's Best'. Edging towards the window, he stared outside into the blackness above the garden and slowly drew the curtains together. The boy remained motionless.

'Hmm. Didn't know you were suddenly interested in football Dan?'

In the silence that followed, he took hold of a small swivel chair next to a desk where geometric patterns in garish colours whirled silently in the cyberspace of a computer screen saver. Drawing the black metallic chair near to the bed he slumped down on it, feeling it creak and wobble beneath him.

'So who's your favourite Boro player, then?' he enquired.

'Haven't got one really. But if I did it would be him'.

Daniel held up the pages of the book towards his father, to reveal a head and shoulders photograph of a player called George Camsell. Richard quickly studied the text.

'But he was playing donkeys years ago. Why him?'

'Did you see him play?'

Richard feigned a look of anger, and flicked his right hand about Daniels ear.

'Cheeky monkey' he snarled.

The ice broken, Richard took the book from his sons grasp and smiled.

'Well, I must admit he had a great scoring record according to this' he murmured, scanning through the pages, 'fifty nine league goals in thirty nine games'.

'Did Granddad ever see him play, do you think?' Daniel beamed.

'Maybe, but I can't remember your Granddad ever talking about things like footy.'

'1927 Top scorer Dad' the boy observed, a matter-of-fact expression on his young face.

'You are a funny little sod' replied his father.

'He used to dribble past the other players like this.' Daniel rose suddenly from the bed and performed a dance like routine across the carpet, an imaginary ball at his feet.

'How do you know that then ?'

There was a moment of quietness when Richard felt that the boy had retreated again. 'Dunno, someone told me I suppose'.

'Not Phil I bet. He wouldn't have a clue about anybody who doesn't play for Man United. Specially not an old player like George Camsell'.

Daniel gave a long sigh.

'But Dad, he wasn't old when he was playing'.

Richard chuckled 'Quite right son'. He paused .

'Can't you remember who it was?'

Daniel turned his face to the window and sighed again, while Richard nervously swivelled around on the small chair.

'How was school today?'

Daniel shrugged, and his father knew the moment had passed. Rising from the chair he came up behind his son and wrapped his arms around him, kissing him gently on the top of his head. The boy remained rigid and quiet.

'Come on. Let's have something to eat,' Richard whispered as he led him towards the bedroom door. As they entered the landing, he felt Daniel pull back slightly.

'When are we going to see Granddad?'

'Sunday probably....why ?'

'Good,' replied the boy.

It was a question of damage limitation, of course. My spontaneous act of celebration when I had kicked that perfectly round pebble across the ground we had laboured over for so long, had somehow threatened to break a spell and sever the bonds which bound together our little tribe of brothers. I hadn't understood it, but Jesse had.

Now, the sun glinted fiercely off its shiny surface as I toyed with it, gently tossing it between my hands as I crouched on the top step before our front door.

Two young children burst out of the house next door, into the warm sunlight, whooping and yelling as they skipped along the pavement. Several minutes later, the front door of Joey's house opened and his mother emerged, a tiny woman with her hair tied back in a tight bun, carrying a small child in her arms, her seventh. She waited on the pavement for her husband who gently negotiated a large black pram down the front steps, took the baby from his wife and placed the child carefully in the pram as she raised up the concertina hood to protect him from the bright sunlight. She hooked her hand round her husbands arm and as they approached me she smiled and called out 'Ello honey, what've you got there ?'

I managed a thin smile, the pebble slipping from my fingers.

Joey's Dad was a tall man with a strong, kind face dominated by a straight Roman nose. 'You not with the others today Tommy?' he enquired.

I glanced up at them and slid forward to retrieve my pebble.

'They're all round at our house, son. Go on. Get yourself round there. Go on....I dunno...go on now.'

The couple chuckled to each other and stepped aside on the pavement as if inviting me to make my move as I slowly eased myself up, thrust the pebble deep into my pocket and set off for their house.

I loved Joey's house because their living room at the back was always full of happy laughter and even now I could hear our Bill's voice, and Joey's, and those of his two eldest sisters.

I climbed the steps and gently pushed open the front door, tip toeing to the sanctuary of their best room, a place I had never been. All of our houses had a best room which was usually reserved for adults, Sundays only, when the fire would be lit in case of visitors.

The long green sofa seemed more inviting than its partner armchairs, one low, the other high backed, or the four straight backed chairs which faced the centrepiece of the room: an ornate pedal organ. Directly opposite the long sofa upon which I settled, the velvet soft against my young legs, was the multi coloured mantelpiece bedecked by an intricately ornate piece of wooden carving into which decorative little ledges and an oval mirror had been cut. Tall vases and a striking clock had been carefully positioned atop the mantelpiece.

At the base of the fireplace was a deep brass fender with various irons of curious shapes and sizes, a long poker, a rake, tongs and a shovel and brush.

My eyes wandered to the ceiling where the large gaslight was identical to the one in our house, and then down to the picture rail from which a series of enormous pictures had been suspended by cords. The largest of these was framed in gold and depicted a disquieting scene of Scottish cattle which had come down from the mountains to drink at a stream, their large horns reflected in the water. On the opposite wall, in a sunny country lane which resembled countryside totally foreign to the familiar lanes which surrounded our village, a young farm hand was backing some shire horses into a four wheeled wagon.

My attention was distracted by a familiar sound from outside, coming from the direction of Church End Farm. I sprung to the bay window and peered out through the net curtains, to be rewarded by the sight of the grocery van of Henry Eldon Fletcher, his name emblazoned on a white canvas awning built on top of the chassis, fresh from its climb up the bank and now on its way towards Chiltons Avenue and beyond. I loved the sight and sound of that van, especially in the cold winter months when Mister Fletcher would buy paraffin from the Danby sisters shop to fill the lamps which clung to the van sides, a precautionary replacement for the front headlight bulbs which often popped with the strain of a steep climb and hard revving of the engine. It trundled past, two of the Eldon brothers in the front open cab, bouncing above the hard spoked wheels, smaller at the front than at the back. From the bay window, I followed its progress as far as I could and was about to withdraw back to the comfort of the sofa when my eyes fixed on a tall, angular, figure resting against a tree on the grassy verge opposite our row of houses. He wore a large cap pulled low so that I could see nothing of his face except for a large, dark moustache. At his feet, I could make out the shape of a grey haversack, while his boots, trousers, rough jacket and shirt all seemed to be of the same light brown colour, as though he was covered in a layer of sawdust. Only his dark moustache and the strange manner in which he rested against the tree, occasionally kicking its narrow trunk, suggested anything of youthfulness.

I was sure that he hadn't been there for any more than a few minutes, or I would surely have noticed him from our front step.

Slowly, the figure stretched and bent down to grab at one of the straps of his haversack which he casually slung over his right shoulder before emerging from the shade of the tree to cross over the road, towards the village green. From the sureness of his stride, I determined that he was probably a young man, perhaps not much older than a boy.

The best room door swung open, heralding a rush of cool air followed by Joey's eldest sister, Joyce. Her natural kindly expression, framed by curly black hair, was a fortunate inheritance of her father and I was strangely reassured by her hushed, urgent whisper as the door clicked shut behind her.

'Tommy Devlin, you shouldn't be in here. Come away from that window.'

I turned back to the net curtain, but the figure was gone.

'You better not have marked our Mam's sofa,'

Trying my broadest grin, I replied 'I thought it was your Dads.'

'Cheeky little beggar' she smiled as she ushered me away from the net curtains towards the middle of the room, 'Have you moved anything?'

'No, I was just looking, honest. I come to see if our Bill was here.'

Joyce gave the furniture a cursory inspection and finding nothing amiss, fixed me with a stare for a few seconds before jerking her thumb in the direction of the back of the house 'They're in there.'

I could hear the familiar laughter of our Bill and Joey as Joyce's hand prodded the small of my back, edging me slowly towards the passage. At the door threshold, my brain debated whether to stand there or run, and delayed its decision a moment too long. I turned to escape but Joyce was quicker and blocked my way.

'Here's the little Devlin' she chuckled, her hands resting on my shoulders from behind as she eased me into the room. Both boys smiled across at me from the kitchen table and I felt a tiny surge of confidence flow down from the top of my head, through my ears to my throat. They had been too hard on me, and had seen the error of their ways, sorry but too pig-headed to say so. They wanted to make up, that was it.

'Well, look what the cat dragged in', grinned Joey.

There were a few seconds of awkward silence before a familiar voice carried from the yard.

'How about going to Dugards?'

Jesse slid round the corner of the back door and stood in the frame, his blue eyes and easy smile lighting up the scene.

Bill then began a curious dance as he thrust his right hand deep into the pocket at the back of his shorts, twisting his neck around to withdraw the contents of a small handful of coppers which he placed, gleefully, on the table. Joey followed suit. Then Jesse walked into the room and placed his contribution on the table.

The three of them watched intently as my sweaty fingers fumbled around in my left pocket, the pebble rattling against a couple of coins.

'Come on man, give,' grinned our Bill, as I slowly managed to extract the coins and place them, triumphantly, next to the others.

Jesse gave me a wink, scooped them all up and handed them to Joey.

We left Joyce to her chores and ran through the yard, out to the green.

Dugards was one of the small 'two up and two down' terrace houses, which fringed the village green facing our school. The front door opened into the parlour which had a counter where, every week day, at any time of the day, the Dugards sold sweets, lemonade, monkey nuts, home made toffee, cigarettes and tobacco. When they closed it on a Saturday night, all the goods in the shop were cleared away including the shelf in the window which always supported boxes of sweets. Then the lace curtains were put up and it became a family sitting room again, for Sundays only.

Our small haul of coins was traded for a bottle of lemonade and a large bag of monkey nuts. The conversation was sparse as we settled on a shady spot under the row of trees opposite the school, a few yards from the Salutation Inn, taking turns to swig from the bottle, the grass at our feet littered with the empty shells of dozens of monkey nuts.

Men came and went from the Salutation, and the Black Horse, further down the green. Some sauntered over to Charlie Pool's to inspect the latest motorcycles lined up outside his garage, while others walked across to the west row side of the green to watch the older boys playing football.

'Our Dad says he don't recognise most of the fellas knocking about here these days' said Joey, now lying on his back with his hands clasped over his stomach. I raised myself up from my squatting position and surveyed the scene, pointing out characters with familiar faces.

'I know im and im, and that fella there, and im, and there's Stanley's dad, and old man Atkinson and...'

Bill's hand grabbed my collar and yanked me down to ground level.

'Says it's the factory. The Synthetic. ICI and that. Bringing them 'ere for the work,' Joey continued.

'Are you gonna work at the factory our Bill, when you're done over there?' I nodded in the direction of our little redbrick school.

'Dunno, mebbe I will, mebbe not. Might work on the railway like Joey's Dad. Or drive a van like Fletcher's. Might be a footballer and play for the Boro.' That brought the conversation to a temporary hiatus as we paused to contemplate what the future might hold for each of us.

Then Jesse piped up, 'Bet you don't know him.'

We all sat up and looked around, quizzically.

'Who you looking at, Jesse?' I asked.

'Over there, in the church gate,' Jesse replied, his eyes fixed on the large roofed lych gate which stood directly opposite the village cross, at the entrance to the churchyard of Saint Cuthberts. The seats on either side of the lych gate, where the coffins traditionally rested before funeral services, were always shrouded in dark shadows under the canopy of the structure. A tall figure was silhouetted under the roof and, even before he strode out into the sunlight, I immediately recognised him as the man I had glimpsed from the bay window of Joey's front room.

His haversack was still slung over his shoulder, and his cap still pulled low over his brow as he pulled up the collar of his jacket and slowly walked across the road to the pedestal of the village cross, then casually threw his load onto the top step where he found a suitable resting place. Reaching for his haversack, he brought out a tin which he rested on his knees while he removed a small pipe from the inside pocket of his sawdust brown jacket. Moments later, a small whiff of white smoke rose from the pipe.

'Who is he, then?' enquired Bill.

Jesse simply replied 'I wonder.'

'Do you think he's come lookin' for work, like them others?' asked Joey.

No one responded. All that we knew and believed went unspoken. None of the young men from our parts would take their rest in the lych gate, or light up a pipe on the steps of the village cross. Those looking for jobs wouldn't be wasting their time in the sunshine. They'd be in the pubs sounding out the locals, or up Belasis Lane at the factory. It had to be a stranger, maybe from another county, far away from here.

The Latimers' silver Audi estate car eased to a gentle stop, its front bumper nudging a bright red azalea bush set in a raised bed of shrubs at the far end of the small car park. Philip and Daniel got out first, and immediately the elder boy knelt on one knee to fasten the lace of his left trainer, his Manchester United baseball cap turned back to front. Fiona, then Richard, were next.

Daniel led the way to the entrance past a long row of identical square windows, some bedecked with lacy curtains, others more stark and bare; some displaying little ornaments and photo frames on their sills, others the odd vase or religious figurine. Beyond the row of square windows were two larger ones, behind which smiling women in white overalls were busy preparing food.

A hanging basket containing two bright red geraniums and some trailing lobelia had recently been suspended from a green bracket at the side of the glass, and beneath it was a small white button set in a metal plate which invited visitors to press and wait. Daniel pressed the button and, seconds later, a tiny old lady shuffled into view and reached behind a panel to press a switch to release the door lock.

'Roy's upstairs in the big room' she beamed, as the family entered.

'Thanks Peggy. How are you today?' Richard enquired.

Ignoring the question, she reached out a stick like arm to gently stroke Philips hand.

He smiled down at her while Daniel stiffened behind him.

'What big boys you are' Peggy grinned, and clapped her hands in delight.

Daniel studiously ignored her and marched towards the lift to the upstairs floor, holding the doors open while the others signed their names in the visitors book. His eyes floated over a couple of typed notices produced on pink A4 paper, stuck with tape to the side of the lift.

GEMMA FROST…CHIROPODIST, EVERY TUESDAY AT TEN

JANEY JAMES WILL SING SONGS FROM THE SHOWS AT THE THURSDAY SING-ALONG COFFEE MORNING…ALL WELCOME

The big room contained four round dining tables with four places set at each, a welsh dresser, a tiny kitchen area where drinks could be made and, adjacent to a ceiling-to-floor window, were two cream sofas and a group of dusty pink armchairs, all occupied. Richard's father Roy was sat in the chair nearest to a huge grey and silver television set showing a video recording of Kramer versus Kramer. He was the last of the residents to notice the arrival of his family, but when recognition finally came to him, he smiled gently and offered a polite handshake to his son.

The boys stood to one side as Fiona stepped forward to kiss Roy on the cheek, until Philip took off his baseball cap and cut in,

' Cor its so hot in here Granddad, I'm boiling,' he declared

'Would you like a drink?' enquired Roy.

The boys followed their grandfather to the kitchen and watched patiently as he rummaged through a wall cupboard in search of two tumblers into which he poured some orange juice and water.

'He looks quite well, really' observed Fiona, quietly.

A stout girl in a white uniform who was gathering up some magazines which had been scattered over one of the cream sofas, smiled broadly at Richard, then mouthed at him in a low, whispering voice 'He's always a bit quiet, but he's no bother, really.'

Richard stared intently at the small scene as the boys finished off the orange juice in a few seconds and Philip returned to his parents side, leaving Daniel alone with Roy, the two of them engaged his grandfather in some small conversation.

'Would you credit it?' His voice sounded heavy and sad. 'Look at the two of them. I could never talk to my father like that. Now I struggle to talk to my son.'

Fiona grasped his arm and gently squeezed it. 'Come on darling. Let's see if we can get them outside for a little while.'

The garden at Airdale Lodge was approached via a wooden gate at the side of the main building and was divided into two areas, both comprising of a circular path surrounding a lawned area with shrubs planted here and there in small clumps. In one corner, nearest to the residents rooms, was a small patio where shade was provided by three green sun umbrellas, attached to small round, wooden tables and surrounded by a tiny cluster of loungers and reclining deckchairs. At the furthest corner from the building, a short path led to a wooden ramp and a round pergola with a bench seat inside. Two wind chimes were attached to the roof of the pergola; one with four softly chiming metal rods, the other with six bamboo rods.

The Latimers formed a slow procession around the lawn with Roy at the head, supported by the two boys on either arm, Fiona in a large blue sun hat and wrap around sun glasses slightly behind and Richard bringing up the rear, arms folded behind his back. Every couple of yards, the procession would stop while Roy pointed out a different aspect of the garden until they arrived at the patio where small pleasantries were exchanged with one or two residents sat under the umbrellas.

'Dad, I need to get something from the car' exclaimed Philip.

Richard removed the keys to the Audi from his trouser pocket and dangled them in front of his son.

'Don't be long, don't start the car and DO NOT play around with the sound system...especially my CDs.'

'Promise' replied the boy as he took the keys and made off in the direction of the car park, to the amusement of one of the ladies under the umbrellas.

'I remember when I could run that fast' she chuckled, 'They have such energy at that age and it's so lovely to see them. You do very well to bring them here, you really do, some wouldn't bother you know.'

Fiona smiled at the old lady 'I think Richard's father appreciates it, and the boys like to see him.'

'Yes, I'm sure he does. Roy is a quiet chap. Doesn't say much, but your visit will make his day. He's very fortunate to have a family who care for him.'

'Do you have many visitors, Mrs......?' enquired Richard.

'Darling' interjected Fiona.

'Please. Don't fuss. It's Miss actually, and no, I don't have many family visitors but I do get the occasional person who remembers me from school. I used to be a schoolmistress you see. Mary Thompson. How nice to meet you.' She held out her hand to Richard.

'It must be rewarding when people remember you.'

'They bring their children sometimes, you know. That's lovely. Of course, I remember when they themselves were young. As if it was yesterday.' She glanced over Fiona's shoulder towards the far corner of the garden, where Daniel and his grandfather had reached the pergola in which a single figure occupied the tiny bench seat in the shade of its canopy. Daniel led his grandfather by the hand up the short path to the round wooden structure.

'Well. There's a thing,' declared Mary.

Fiona spun round to follow the old lady's line of vision.

'What is it, Miss Thompson?' she breathed.

'Please, do call me Mary my dear.' She paused. 'Sorry if I alarmed you, it's nothing at all. Just that...well how can I put this? Your little chap there must be quite a persuasive child. I'm afraid some old folk are not, well, perhaps not the friendliest of people and so…well…your father-in-law Roy is rather withdrawn at times and, oh I don't know… to see him walking over for chat with….' She stopped. 'Really, I've said enough, silly old fool that I am. I really shouldn't be so judgemental about people. Frightful of me.' At that moment, a young woman in blue uniform walked out from the building into the sunshine, carrying a jug of orange juice.

'A cool drink Mary? What about you Elsie? Jack?'

Miss Thompson retreated to the shade of one of the sun parasols.

Fiona called after her 'Mary? Who are they talking to over there?'

The old lady waved a thin arm 'Please, don't mind me. It's nothing and nobody, my dear.'

'Would you like a drink Mrs Latimer?' enquired the young woman in the uniform.

Fiona and Richard each took a glass of orange juice from her.

'We try to get our residents to mix together but, of course, some prefer their own company and that's fine. The men are less sociable than the women, on the whole, and some are very private.' Her voice was almost a whisper.

'Like my father I suppose?' asked Richard.

'Some more than others,' she added, nodding in the direction of the pergola before returning to the main building.

Richard and Fiona stood in silence, occasionally sipping from their glasses, sometimes glancing over towards Daniel, still engaged in conversation with the two old men. It was several minutes before they ambled around the lawn towards the pergola. As they approached, Phillip appeared from the side gate.

'When are we going?' he asked, impassively.

'Now' came the reply from his father.

Phillip surveyed the scene, 'What's he doing? Who's that they're talking to?'

'How would we know?' His mother's voice was terse.

'What a wally. He really gets on my wires sometimes. He's weird my brother. Look at him. Prattling away to a couple of old geezers.' Phillip's cheeks and neck were now flushed from a combination of heat and frustration.

'One of those old geezers happens to be your grandfather' observed his mother.

His head lowered as he mumbled 'I meant the other one.'

Daniel led Roy by the hand towards the rest of his family, and turned his head to glance back at the pergola where the original occupant sat motionless, gazing up at the chimes which softly rattled a melody of random notes into the afternoon air.

'Strange chap,' said Roy. 'Never says much to anybody. In fact that's as much as I've ever heard him talk in one go.'

Richard placed his hand on Daniel's shoulder. 'OK mate?'

Daniel searched his father's eyes, a fleeting expression of concern on his young face. Roy interjected.

'You know me and sport, Richard. Never really took anything up except a spot of sailing that time your mother and I took you to Dorset. Do you remember? Certainly not football. Switch it off when it comes on the television.'

'You mean you were talking about football, Dad?'

'Not me exactly. Daniel. Wanted to know about someone who played for Middlesbrough.'

Richard stiffened. 'George Camsell.'

'Who?' snapped Phillip.

Roy's eyebrows rose 'That's right. How did you know?'

'Daniel's told me about him, haven't you son.'

'Well, he seemed to know far more than I.' Roy beamed down at his grandson.

Richard seemed to relax a little. 'Did the old gentleman fill in any gaps, son?'

Daniel gave a half smile and nodded gently.

'And he said he would he tell me more if I come another time.'

'Wally' said Phillip.

Fiona gathered up her family and led them all to the side gate from where they could walk slowly back to the main entrance to say their farewells to Roy. As they turned the corner, the chimes were offering another softer song in the pergola, which was empty once more.

The Bottoms were alive with tiny creatures, voles, water rats, frogs, toads, harvest mice, flies and small boys.

Days remained long and warm, the only rain coming from infrequent, short showers brought in from the light westerly clouds which rode mischievously on the back of the gentle breeze that flitted across the valley of the Tees. It darted here and there over its tributaries and streams, and later in the evenings brought a cool chill of surprise to the earth, leaving a damp dew to be steamed off by the following morning's sun.

From our house in South View, we could walk a few yards to the old duck pond and cross over into Mill Lane, a long track which meandered for two or three miles down towards the Haverton Hill road close to the banks of the Tees. New houses had sprung up on one side of Mill Lane, in a small estate between our village and the chemical factory, the names of the roads often resembling those of rural idylls such as Rydal and Wooller. They were built quickly and cheaply by the Synthetic to house the influx of new migrant workers, but, nevertheless boasted three or four bedrooms, a downstairs bathroom, and electric heating. The land on the other side of the road was open fields, formerly owned by the Atkinson family who ran Brooke House Farm, and recently sold off to developers.

Joe's best pal, Les Cannon had told him that when he had been walking the lane a few days ago, his uncle Ned Wilkinson had told him that they were going to build a row of shops along the road, so that people could buy all the things they needed in one place. When Bill and I told our parents, my father declared that it was about time too, but my mother raised herself up from her chair by the window and said simply "fancy", before retreating to the back yard where she remained for the next ten minutes.

Brook House Farm was a mile away, where the westerly aspect of Mill Lane opened up to reveal a landscape that had remained unchanged for centuries, where the fields sloped away down to the banks of Billingham Beck, and eventually to the river itself, all set against the far away backdrop of the Cleveland Hills.

As soon as I had been able to walk any reasonable distance as a child, I had been to those fields, along those winding footpaths and tracks, sometimes in a family group, sometimes with neighbours who often led fishing parties of children armed with nets and jars. It was the most glorious place on earth.

That afternoon, Bill, Joe, Jesse and I had walked through one of the fields, along a footpath which took us past the farm, where two of the Atkinson boys, Cyril and Percy, were playing with a small Jack Russell dog in the farmyard. They took little persuasion to join us, on through the meadows and between the hedgerows to the footbridges over the old mill race and across Billingham Beck.

When we had reached the other side of the footbridge, we crouched in a circle on the far bank, with the Atkinson's little dog in the centre, scampering excitedly to each boy for attention, and licking at our feet. As I looked back across at the mill buildings, a thin line of washing caught my eye. My mother still referred to it as Moon's Mill from the days of its final miller at the turn of the century, Francis Moon. Though it was still inhabited by one of the Brooke House farm labourers, it had long ago ceased to operate as a corn mill and the water wheel, sluice and tail race were in the final stages of decay, while the walls of the outbuildings had been allowed to go unrepaired.

Yet, to Bill and I, the old buildings remained what they had always been: a magnificent fortress of the imagination, the sheriff's castle at Nottingham, ready to be captured by Robin Hood and his gang, or Camelot where the knights of the Round Table assembled every morning around the time we were getting ready for school.

On such a day as this, with the shadows starting to lengthen and form dramatic shapes, black and deep on the crusty red brick of its crumbling walls, the old mill had become Fort Laramie, where Tom Mix and his pals would battle for supremacy over Sitting Bull, among the cactus plants and covered wagons on either side of the beck.

It was a game of stealth and ambush as we broke up into pairs, hiding from each other, ducking and diving among the grasses and reeds surrounding the outbuildings of the mill, revealing ourselves only to fire off imaginary bullets and arrows. The little Jack Russell scampered around in the grass, following whatever scent took his fancy until, after half an hour or so, Cyril emerged from a reed patch to call him from his latest quarry.

'Here boy,....here Skip.....come on boy!'

Cyril repeated his call. Several long seconds later, there was no sign of Skip.

'Here boy.....Here Skip' cried his brother Percy.

Joe, who had been stalking behind a hawthorn bush, came out into the open to join the brothers as, one by one, we slipped away from our hiding places and began calling for the dog.

Cyril called out 'Where is he, the little bugger? Come round to the bridge, see if we can spot him from there.'

We followed the order and stood in a line on the footbridge to scan the terrain.

'We could split up and go round the mill an' that, and shout out if we find him' suggested Bill. Heads were nodded in agreement and we started to fan outwards from the bridge, shouting out for Skip, when Jesse's voice rose above us.

'Wait, come back a minute.'

'What's up now' I enquired, irritated by the delay.

'Look' replied Jesse, his right arm pointing in the direction of the long grass near to the outbuildings of the old mill.

We returned to the bridge and scanned the scene.

'Can't see nowt' whispered Percy, his eyes now filling with tears, his face flushed and distraught.

Jesse pulled Percy towards him till their heads were touching,

'Follow my arm' he said.

We all glanced up at the pair of them, to make sure we were looking in the right direction and followed Jesse's arm and forefinger until, there, just visible, was a light column of wispy white smoke rising from the long grass.

I could feel my throat tighten with excitement 'What is it, Jesse?'

'Come on, stay close. Let's take a look' he replied.

We grouped ourselves into a tight pack and edged forward until we were within twenty feet of the source of the smoke, stopping silently and abruptly at the raising of Jesse's right hand.

There was some movement from the grass, followed by a cough, then a tall figure cast a dark shadow across the red bricks of the outhouse as it slowly raised itself up. The figure had his back to us but began to turn in the half light, his pipe still firmly in his mouth, his arms gently cradling the little Jack Russell before softly placing him on the ground.

The man's voice was ponderous 'This who yer lookin for?'

Skippy barked once and trotted calmly over to Percy who scooped him up and handed him on to Cyril, before we all took it in turns to cuddle the tiny dog.

Only Jesse remained still, his clear blue eyes fixed on the stranger, who's large cap and dark moustache immediately distinguished him as the man in the lych gate.

'It's him. That fella sat on the cross, you know, outside the pub, on the….'

'Shut up our Tommy,' I felt Bill's hand swipe past my right ear.

In the silence that followed, white clouds of thin smoke continued to rise from the stranger's pipe as he stood motionless in the half light.

'Put the dog down, Percy' said Jesse.

Percy looked anxiously at Jesse who's eyes had not diverted their gaze, and gently lowered Skip down onto the wooden deck of the footbridge. The little dog sniffed at his feet then trotted onto the path and through the grass towards the man who bent forward to receive him and, as he did so, the large cap slipped off his head into the ground. When the stranger had straightened up, he took a few steps forward with Skip in his arms once more, bringing a collective gasp from the footbridge.

I looked along the line of faces, mask like with eyes wide betraying a curious mixture of fear and curiosity.

The strangers dark hair covered only half of his scalp, the other half was red and bare, the raw skin dominated by a deep, furrowed scar which ran from the crown of his head, down over his brow towards his left eye socket, which was empty and closed.

'Look at im,' this time Bill's hand found its target and I winced in pain.

'If we go as if we're walking back home, maybe Skip'll follow us,' suggested Joe.

'Not going without him,' sniffed Percy.

'No. Not without him,' agreed Cyril.

We all seemed to sense that if one of us was to bolt and run off through the fields, back to Mill Lane and the sanctuary of home, the others would surely follow at his heels. Instead, we were rooted to the wooden boards of that old footbridge.

Except for Jesse.

Wiping his hands down the sides of his trousers, he edged forward from the bridge until he was a yard from the stranger who gave Skip a small kiss on the snout before handing him over. Jesse ruffled the dog's ears and placed him back on the ground where he scurried back to Percy and Cyril.

I called over 'We're going home now Jesse, come on.'

He turned to face me and the rest. 'Without saying thanks?'

Cyril muttered a barely audible 'Ta', followed by Percy and Bill.

A broad grin spread over Jesse's face as he waved us over towards himself and the stranger, 'You can say it properly, can't you?'

We shuffled towards the pair of them as Skip rushed around at our feet, circling between our legs and licking at the stranger's shoes.

41

'Grand little fella. What do you call him?' His voice was warm and calm.

'Skip,' replied Percy 'He's a Jack Russell.'

'That he is, lad. That he is.'

'He doesn't run off all the time. Not like just now,' said Cyril.

The stranger smiled and placed his pipe to his lips.

'Happen he just got a bit curious. Jack Russell's are like that.'

'Have you got a dog, mister?' enquired Joe.

'Did have once' he replied through a cloud of white smoke.

Joe continued 'What happened to im?'

'Died' came his simple response, the livid scar almost glowing in the twilight, emphasising the deep, dark hollow of his empty eye socket.

I remember looking up at my brother and seeing an expression I didn't recognise, a strange sort of combination of pity, disgust and curiosity as he averted his eyes from the stranger's gaze towards mine, 'Are we going home now, our Bill?' I asked him.

The man removed his pipe from his mouth 'Reckon your folks'll be starting to wonder what you're up to.'

We turned to take our leave when Jesse replied, 'Where's your home? We haven't seen you round here before.'

'Out Whitby way....here...know what this is?' he fished in his jacket pocket and brought out a small black object no more than an inch high, the shape of a horse's head set on a round base.

'I seen one before,' said Percy, 'Our uncle George, he plays with 'em things, on a board with squares on it.'

'A chess piece,' explained Cyril, 'That's what that is. Like draughts only harder. I seen them playing. Me dad and uncle George.'

The stranger's face broke into a smile. 'Know what it's made of?'

We shook our heads as one.

'Jet. Jet that is. Whitby jet. Black as night,' he grinned.

'Where did you find it?' I asked.

'Made it, young un. Carved it and polished it meself''

Joe had been quiet but stepped forward to take a closer look at the smooth black piece, 'Are you living round here now?'

'Sort of.' He replied.

'In the village?'

'Not exactly.' He turned slightly and moved away towards the wall of the outbuilding where he tapped his pipe against the old bricks.

Jesse spoke, 'Sleeping rough, out here.' It was more of a statement than a question.

'Just till I get some work, lad.'

'Then what?'

Jesse became more animated, 'The factory. Plenty of work. There's men getting work every day. Moving in with their families. Loads of them.'

'Aye. Well, 'appen I'll give it a try then. Maybe tomorrow.'

I started to shiver 'Our Bill. Can we go home now?'

The stranger nodded over to my brother, 'You better get a move on. Go on, get yourselves home. Quickly mind, all of you.'

I felt my shoulders ease with a sense of relief as Percy gathered up Skip and we all turned back towards the footbridge. We were almost there when I heard the stranger calling out to me.

'Here. Young un. Here a minute.'

The others hovered in the grass by the bridge as I looked to Jesse for some reassurance.

'Go on Tommy. It's alright' he whispered.

I felt my legs carry me back towards the old wall of the mill where the man was relighting his pipe and waited for the billows of white smoke to clear and reveal his ravaged face, once more.

'Here. You take this,' he smiled, placing the black horse's head into my hand.

I found myself smiling back, 'Thanks mister,' and ran back to the others. When I turned to wave back to him, he had gone.

In the spacious kitchen of the Cedars, everything was as Richard and Fiona had planned. The morning sunlight gleamed off the granite work surfaces and slid gently onto the warmth of the solid oak cabinets and cupboards which stretched comfortably along three sides of the room. Crusty surfaced Italian tiles presented a cool background to the various pots, jars and utensils placed along the tops, and contrasted dramatically with the deep red of the double oven and matching cooker hood which dominated the far wall.

Stone floor tiles, coupled with a series of artificial beams which crossed the ceiling and concealed the tiny halogen lighting units, added to the farmhouse effect, supplemented by the huge wooden table bought at auction by Richard, who now sat at one end of it, cradling a large mug of coffee while his wife sat opposite.

'You have to admit, darling, at least he is starting to communicate a little more' she said, hopeful of a supportive response.

When none came, she stood up and went to the small flat screen television which sat in one corner of the run of granite work surfaces. Picking up the remote control, she flicked through the channel options until BBC radio 2 appeared on the menu chart, at which point she pressed 'select' as the Rolling Stones "Brown Sugar" rebounded off the Italian tiles.

'I suppose they're establishment now' she continued, 'God, I remember when they were, you know, everybody's favourite..'

'Fee, please. Just turn it down.' Richard's voice was sharp and tense.

'..Monsters. Mick the devil incarnate' she sighed wearily, pressing at the remote until the sound was little more than a tinkling jingle.

'I suppose you're right' he replied.

'I always liked Charlie best, but Theresa thought he was the ugliest man she'd ever seen.' Her smile froze as Richard's eyes narrowed.

He placed the mug down with a deliberation that suggested hostility.

'What?' he spat. 'What?'

She returned to her chair, 'Charlie Watts. The drummer.'

'I know who Charlie bloody Watts is, for God's sake. Fiona. I'm talking about our son. You know. Our youngest. You know, the weird little kid who only seems to come alive when he's talking to his granddad or some other old creep?"

'Where the hell did that come from?'

He leaned forward over the table and, as his elbows thumped on the broad surface of the kitchen table, buried his face in his hands and mumbled a barely audible apology through his fingers.

'What for?' Fiona demanded.

'Mmmm?' he groaned.

'You're sorry for what exactly, Richard? For calling our son a weirdo, or implying that your father is an old creep?'

His shoulders rose as he inhaled deeply, and placed his palms face down on the table, his eyes drawn and lined.

Fiona reached across and touched the tips of his fingers with her own.

'Talk to him, Richard' she said.

He sighed 'I've tried Fee. You know I have. It's always the same. Just as I feel I'm, I don't know, connecting, or bonding or whatever those quacks call it, he just seems to…freeze me out somehow. Wants to retreat. To be with…..'

'His imaginary friend' she spoke the words slowly and blandly 'But, darling, we must try to do what Cartner advised. Keep talking and keep trying. You'll see. Keep trying. It's a phase. I know it's just a phase. Growing up. He'll come out of it.'

'I know' his thin smiled betrayed his lack of faith in his wife's prognosis. 'But it's so hard.'

She took his hands in hers across the table 'Why don't you talk to him now? About anything. Your work even. Anything.'

He closed his eyes and nodded 'Yup.'

Fiona gave him a wink as he rose slowly from his chair, and listened as his shoes made a sharp, squeaking sound as they crossed the expanse of flooring towards the staircase, becoming softer and more muffled as they reached the landing and the bedroom corridor. Only then did she return to the remote control and the fragile comfort of the radio.

Above her, Richard tapped at the door of Daniel's room and stepped inside. His son was sat at his computer desk, but the machine was not switched on. Daniel was tracing a line with a pencil and ruler as he put the finishing touches to a black and white drawing, his nose inches from the paper, brow creased in fierce concentration, his tongue poking out between his lips in that curious mannerism he had adopted since babyhood.

'Hmm, you look busy. Anything interesting?' he asked, in a voice which seemed louder than he had intended.

Daniel paused, and nodded, not taking his eyes from the drawing.

'School Project?'

Daniel shook his head vigorously.

'May I take a look?'

'Suppose so' replied the boy, taking a careful hold of the top corners of the drawing and lifting it from the surface of the desk and raising it so that his father could inspect it.

'Wow. That's some place. Where is it?' he asked as he inspected Daniel's curious depiction of a tall building set beside a road, with a handful of people grouped around it's base.

Daniel shrugged.

'You made it up? Well done you. We'll make an architect of you yet, Dan.'

The boy gave a hint of a smile, 'When did you start to draw buildings Dad?'

Eager to prolong the theme, Richard exaggerated the effort of recall and took the drawing over to the window to examine it further,

'Oh, I think I was a good bit older than you...and I wasn't as good as you at your age either.'

He paused, 'This is quite interesting, where did you see it? Have you thought it up out of your head?' He regretted the question as soon as it had left his lips and tried to change tack. 'Have you thought about where the entrance door would be?'

'It's finished' said Daniel.

Richard placed the drawing back on the desk and pushed his hands deep into his pockets, 'Well, it's very good. You should keep this up you know, keep practising. I think you must take after me.'

He was about to change the subject when Daniel picked up the drawing.

'It's round the back, I think' he exclaimed.

His father's bemused expression prompted him to continue.

'I think that's where it would be' he went on.

'Oh...I see. Well, you should know. It's your drawing' Richard replied.

'I know, but....Well....It has to be right. I want it to be right.'

Richard knelt down on the carpet in front of the desk and took hold of the drawing again, this time placing it on the floor which he patted twice, as a signal for Daniel to squat beside him.

'Let's see. The door could be round the back of the house' he ventured, "Or it could be at the side. It's certainly a tall looking house. How many floors do you think?"

Daniel was silent for a few seconds. 'Four, counting the one at the very top.'

'Four. And what do you think the inside would be like?' he went on, 'It looks like....well...I don't know. It's certainly not modern in concept.'

'What's concept mean?'

'It means an idea. The design. It's traditional. With small regular windows and a pitched roof.'

'Pitched?'

'Sloping. Not flat,' observed Richard 'Who would live here, do you think?'

'It's empty. No one lives there,' replied the boy.

Richard started to laugh, 'You mean you've designed a house for nobody to live in?'

Daniel gave a soft little giggle, 'Kind of. The idea just sort of...came into my head and I kept on drawing it until it was finished.'

As they laughed together for the first time in months, Richard fought to stem tears of emotion as he shared the precious moment with his son.

'You should take it to show your granddad,' he said.

'Can I ? ....Don't you mind?'

'Of course not. Why would I mind? Daniel, you should show him this. It's really good. Honestly, I'm not just saying it. You've drawn it well. He'll be interested. Take it, next time we go.'

'Right then, I will. Only, I thought....'

'What, son? What did you think?'

'Well. I thought you and Mum didn't like it much when we go to see Granddad and I talk to him a lot. I thought it kind of made you cross.'

Richard smiled and hugged Daniel. 'No way. No way. You talk to Granddad all you want. And to me. About anything. Anything you like.'

The tinny, rattling sound coming from the earphones of Philip's new ipod could clearly be heard through the warm Sunday afternoon air as the Latimers stepped out from their Peugeot into the car park. Courteous nods and smiles were exchanged between Richard and Fiona and two of the wheelchair-bound residents who had been pushed out into the forecourt to enjoy a spot of people watching.

Philip's shoulders and hips occasionally shuffled in time with the rhythms penetrating his ears, while his lips silently mouthed obscure lyrics.

Daniel walked stiffly, slightly behind the others, as he took in the scene and surveyed the way ahead, seemingly anxious to guard the large, parcel shaped object carried under his right arm. Slowly, he trailed them along the familiar route, past the visitors book and the dispenser of antiseptic cream, across the foyer to the lift.

'I'll follow you up' he said to the others, peering inside and shifting his weight from one foot to the other.

His mother edged further back into the small space, squashing against the other two to make room for him.

Daniel hesitated for a few seconds.

'Don't be silly. Get in. No one's going to bump it' she smiled.

Philip removed his ear pieces and hung them around his neck 'What's happening?'

Daniel, still gripping the parcel under his right arm, turned a full half circle so that he was facing the far wall of the foyer, and slowly reversed into the lift. As the doors closed in front of his upturned nose, he heard his brother's flat voice from behind,

'Wimp.'

The lift doors opened onto a small landing which afforded a clear view, through glass panels into the lounge area where a handful of residents were dozing in front of the large television. Roy was not among them.

To the left were the double doors to the lounge, and beyond were a large notice board, a small sitting area, and a corridor of rooms. To the immediate right of the lift was a store cupboard and a glass door which led on to another corridor of rooms, the first of which was number 43 which belonged to Roy.

Richard steered his family through the glass door entrance and gently tapped on the door three times, and opened it a few inches.

'Dad?' he whispered, 'Dad? It's Richard.'

After a few seconds, he opened the door a little further, 'Fiona and the boys are here.'

He glanced across the empty room to the far wall where a gold framed photograph of his smiling mother, taken on holiday in Majorca ten years earlier, beamed down at the neat, single bed, next to which Roy's red dressing gown was draped over a pale blue armchair. At the other side of the bed, a white alarm clock perched on top of a set of three pine effect drawers, behind it was a framed photograph of Richard dressed in his graduation gown. Smaller photographs of Fiona and the boys adorned the small dressing table next to the matching pine wardrobe.

'Dad?' he called out softly as he opened the door to the small en suite bathroom, his eyes quickly taking in the row of four toilet rolls, the electric razor neatly folded away in its case, the toothbrush propped up inside the tall, glass tumbler next to the toothpaste for sensitive gums.

A foreign voice called into the bedroom 'Hello. How are you? Roy is in exercises.'

Fiona and the boys turned to the doorway where a tiny oriental girl in blue uniform smiled broadly at them, 'You wait here for him?'

'Granddad is doing his keep fit...well cool' chuckled Philip.

Fiona made for the door, 'Can we go to see him please? The boys would like that.'

'Sure. They nearly finished. In the far lounge. Not be long now if you want to go see.'

Philip led Fiona and Richard out into the corridor towards the glass porch, leaving

Daniel hovering at the door, still clutching his parcel, 'I'm going to wait here I think.'

His father waved a weary arm as a gesture of permission and, without turning, followed Fiona to the far lounge.

The girl stared intently into Daniel's young eyes.

'You not go with the others?'

Daniel felt the blood rush to his ears as he hovered awkwardly beside Roy's bed, then gently shook his head and shifted his weight from one foot to the other.

Her smile remained broad and fixed, 'You bring something for Roy?'

He looked at her blankly, until she nodded at the parcel.

'Oh. Er no...well, that is not really. It's just something I brought to show him that my Dad said would be, er, that he would um like...because it's of a building and, erm.....' he heard his voice trail off into nothing as the

49

girl stood motionless at the door. He was about to make a bolt for the passage to join the others in the main lounge when she suddenly became distracted and turned away from him into the corridor.

Daniel's curiosity was aroused by the raising of a familiar voice from the next room.

'If you're coming in, then come in for God's sake.'

He followed the girl into the corridor and peered into room 44.

'Thomas, why you don't like the exercise?' she was stood behind the seated figure of the old gentleman who had spoken to him about George Camsell in the garden pergola, her tiny hands resting on his shoulders as he tapped away at a laptop computer.

'Because, my little Tiger Lily, I don't need it, don't want it and prefer my own company in the afternoons thank you very much.' He swivelled in his seat. 'Do what you have to do, but don't touch my desk here, there's a good'un. It's not as if I create much mess in here. Shouldn't take you long. Quick wipe around. Fiddle with the bedclothes. Make sure I haven't peed myself and Bob's your uncle, Fanny's your aunt.'

'Faaaanny?' she mouthed.

'Never mind' he sighed, swivelling back towards the keyboard. As he did so, he caught sight of Daniel whose wide eyes were slowly taking in the books and magazines which occupied a small shelf on the far wall, and the pictures and photographs of local scenes which he recognised from his school books.

'Had a good look?' Thomas enquired briskly.

Daniel replied 'Hello.'

'Hello.'

The girl was fussing around the bed, adjusting the pillows and pulling back the sheets until she eventually broke the ensuing silence.

'This Roy's grandson.'

There was no recognition in Thomas's expression as he stared blankly at Daniel's bowed head while the girl took a cleaning cloth to the window sill, rearranged a pile of magazines and ruffled the curtains.

'I didn't mean to be nosey. Sorry' whispered Daniel.

The boy was disappointed that Thomas had not been more friendly towards him or wanted to resume a conversation and yet, even to his young mind it seemed to him that the worrying frown which creased the old man's brow and made him a little scary seemed to have its roots in a strange sense of frustration and bewilderment on the old man's part, rather than annoyance.

50

'What've you got there? Under your arm?'

'Now you nosey, Thomas,' the girl laughed 'You brought something for your grandfather, Mister Roy?'

'Sort of.'

She smiled at the two of them and tried to change the subject 'You like the football, maybe. Yes? You watch the football? All boys like the football I think'

'Mmmm well sort of ' mumbled Daniel, hoping for a small sign of encouragement from the old man, something that could perhaps lead on to more stories about days long gone.

'Sort of ' replied Thomas, his facing lifting slowly, the eyes brightening as the girl gathered together her cloth and duster, casting a quick glance over her shoulder at the bed before leaving the room.

'Bloody fool' said Thomas.

The words seemed to scatter across Daniel's face like hailstones as he tried, in vain, to hold back the desperate, hot feeling of suffocation and shame that enveloped him as the tears welled in his eyes.

The old man's jaw sagged, as Daniel remained rooted to the spot, 'No, no no. Her, not you' he whispered gently as his left hand beckoned the boy to come closer, while his right buried itself deep into a trouser pocket and extracted a large white handkerchief.

'Blow your nose. Go on. Blow it.'

Daniel took a deep breath and wiped his eyes before following the order.

His voice was barely audible to Thomas, 'You said you would talk to me. I thought. Last time. You told me about, you know, George Camsell and all that stuff.'

Thomas's jaw dropped again as the pain of recall etched itself across his features,

'Yes.......Oh Yes, that's right...' his shoulders drooped as he seemed to shrink into himself, 'Well now. Stop your blubbing then.......I'm sorry.'

Daniel shuffled the parcel around under his arm and readjusted his feet, but was silent.

'It's not your fault, son. It's me. It's my memory. It's what sometimes happens. I'm sorry if I, erm, upset you. I remember you now. Course I do. George Camsell. Mmmm. Sit. Sit down. Go on, son. Sit down on the bed. Put your parcel down somewhere.'

Daniel perched himself on the end of the bed, while Thomas swivelled around until he was square on to the boy, their knees almost touching, the parcel now on the boy's lap like a tray between the two of them. The old man's eyes rested on it.

'Erm. Do you think I could have my hankie back....if you're done with it?'

Daniel removed his right hand from the parcel and delicately manoeuvred it, silently, towards Thomas who took it in his left hand and carefully folded it before pushing it into his trouser pocket.

'I expect your Granddad will be back up in a few minutes. Can't be doing with all that keep fit stuff myself but....takes all sorts.'

Daniel gave a small smile.

'Is it a picture?' Thomas enquired, his eyebrows raised in expectation.

Daniel nodded.

'Something you've done. At school maybe?'

'Not at school' Daniel replied.

The old man raised his voice slightly 'Well give me a bloody clue....I mean. Sorry, I mean....what is it?...if you don't mind me asking.'

Daniel gazed down at the parcel and whispered 'Would you like to see it?'

It was Thomas's turn to be silent for a few seconds before he gave a nod to the boy.

'If you're sure.'

Daniel stood up slowly and sidled round to the side of the bed where he placed the parcel on the pale blue blanket and proceeded to unpick the sticky tape at its edges, before carefully removing the paper wrapping.

Thomas fingers fumbled about on the top of his head until he located his spectacles and pulled them down to his eyes. He placed his hands on his knees and raised himself up from his seat to join Daniel at the bedside.

The drawing of the tall building had been pasted by Richard onto a grey cardboard mount and Daniel, on his father's advice, had signed the bottom right hand corner in his best writing hand.

Outside the room, in the corridor, a trolley was being pushed towards the dining room, but neither the old man nor the boy heard it.

Daniel felt strangely comforted as the warmth of Thomas's hand envelope his own, and he turned his small face upwards to try to gauge the expression on the old man's face. Thomas cleared his throat.

'It's very good son. Very good. Did you do this all by yourself or did someone help you?'

'Well, my Dad pasted it onto the card.'

'Yes, but you did all the drawing, eh?'

'Yes.'

'Yes...it's very good......May I?' asked Thomas, bending down slightly towards the bed to pick up the drawing.

Daniel shoved his hands into his trouser pockets before nodding his assent and Thomas lifted the drawing up to within six inches of his eyes, then carried it gently over towards the window and presented it to the daylight.

'Son, where did you get the idea from? I mean, for the building? Did you get it from a picture?' He brought the drawing back to the bed and laid it down again in its original position on top of the pale blue blanket.

'No. Honestly. No picture. It just sort of came into my head. Honestly.'

A thin shaft of sunlight from the window spread itself like a ribbon across the bed and shone against the brown frames of Thomas's spectacles, behind which the old man's eyes twinkled.

He sensed the boy's discomfort and quietly chuckled at him, 'It's alright. I mean that doesn't matter. It's just that, well, it's....very, very, good....perfect. So I just thought....maybe. Oh I don't know, maybe you saw it somewhere in a book and just remembered what it looked like? Hmmm?'

Daniel hastily removed his hands from his pockets and picked up the drawing, 'No. It was like I said. No picture. You can ask my friend, he was with me when I drew it in my bedroom.....' His voice trailed away into a mumble.

'Your pal eh?'

Familiar voices were approaching along the corridor as Daniel placed the drawing, once more, under his arm and turned to go.

'Sounds like they're back,' said Thomas.

Daniel nodded in silence.

The old man shuffled over to his desk, raised his spectacles up onto the top of his head, slowly sat down and swivelled around to his laptop as if to shut out the rest of the world.

Daniel hovered for a few seconds before his mother's cheerful voice called out

'Where are you, number two son?'

He approached the door, quickly glancing over Thomas's shoulder but the screen of the laptop was still blinking into life and offered no clue as to the object of the old man's interest.

As he left the room, he heard a steady voice from within.

'Thanks for showing me your drawing.'

53

he old cottages, with their stone floors and oil lamps, the pubs, small farms and outbuildings, the tiny shops and the newer terrace houses with their wooden floors and gas lighting; these were still the nucleus of our little world around the green, despite the abundance of signals that heralded upheaval and growth. Change, in itself, was not a concept with which we were unfamiliar. Long ago, there had been no more room for any more housing around the green and our families had witnessed and welcomed the arrival of newer, bigger homes in Wilson Terrace, Stockton Street, Station Road, Parklands Avenue and beyond. Nothing had prepared them, however, for the powerful rate of development which was now taking place all around them. It was as if, suddenly, there were now three separate communities, with different standards of housing, in turn heralding different forms of rivalry.

That Summer, my brother Bill and our pals were largely insensitive to such developments insofar that they rarely intruded into our closed world and, in any case, the messengers of change were usually too obscure for our young senses. Some signs, however, were unmistakeable. The new chemical company had bought up much of the land, including farms. Church End Farm, at the top of the Bank, had been sold off and a new house 'Loriston' had been built on the remaining paddock by Doctor Bowman. My mother considered this to be a true sign of God's work that we had our own doctor living in our village, and him only a few doors away.

Then we picked up, in overheard snatches of conversation, that the Robinsons were to move away from Town End Farm, at the other end of our road in South View, to make way for some new shops at the corner of the junction with Mill Lane, opposite the duck pond. It seemed inconceivable that we would no longer be buying meat from that little shop, with its four steps, where Butcher Alison had taken over from Mister Robinson, who was always referred to by my father and the other men as old 'John Henry.' For over a generation, small boys like us had raced to the slaughter house at the back of the shop, to ask for pig's bladders to be used as substitute footballs on the large green.

In June, my mother had heralded the inauguration of a new priest at Saint Cuthbert's, with great joy. The arrival of such an important figure in the community was greeted with similar enthusiasm by many, but Bill and I escaped the worse of the fuss, perhaps as a result of the outcome of our fishing expedition at the Bottoms and my parent's unfortunate encounter with Miss Elcoat, the lady worker. I remember calling in at Joe's house, the week before the inauguration ceremony, and being shoved by his sister Joyce through the tiny passage into their back yard to witness the taking of a photograph of Joe, with Guy Henderson, both dressed in long black surpluses in preparation for their role in the new church choir. When I raced home to tell the gleeful news to Bill, my mother burst into a lengthy episode of uncontrolled sobbing.

As the weeks rolled on, the grass on the top green had long since turned thin and pale, particularly around the spots which we used for goals, where the grey, parched earth was bare and beginning to crack. The freckles on Jesse's face had become more distinct, and our whole bodies seemed to glow with a light brown radiance, hard and shining at our knees and elbows. Often it was cooler inside than out, but in that wonderful summer, with the assuredness and arrogance of a pride of young lions, we preferred the freedom of our tiny village green where we still ruled supreme.

Long, quiet days began to meander into each other, punctuated only by the sounds of our laughter, our arguments and occasional fights, or the regular chugging of the grocery van and motor cars making their way along the roads and back lanes.

Occasionally, we would be stopped in our tracks by the sudden roar of escaping gas or steam from the direction of the factory, but soon even these interruptions became commonplace and mundane.

When Bill's birthday arrived, there were a couple of extra coins in his trouser pocket; sufficient to enable he and I, Joe and Jesse to share a bag of chips from Lancaster's fish shop. We finished the last of them before we had reached the shade of the large horse chestnut near to the railings on the north side of our school on the little green, and my lips and tongue were now dry and coated from our earlier exertions with a football, and the fatty grease from the chips.

'How much you got left, our Bill?' I enquired, as we approached the tree.

'What's you want to know for?'

With my best pleading voice, I started to protest 'Howay, man. Get a bottle of pop.'

To add some weight of support to my cause, Joe darted in front of my brother and, facing him with his tongue sticking out and panting like a dog, began walking backwards so that Bill could not avoid the clear message.

Unmoved, Bill sat down at the base of the trunk of the horse chestnut and we, naturally, followed suit.

Jesse beamed one of his broadest grins, as Joe and I continued to pant like dogs.

'My birthday. My money' said Bill.

'Mean. Mean. Mean' Joe protested.

I sighed, 'Tight, our Bill. Tight.'

Jesse's laughter rang out and, shoving me on the shoulder, he began to imitate a sobbing child, his shoulders heaving in huge, exaggerated sobs and howls. Enraged and mildly embarrassed, I felt my blood rise.

'Tight our Bill, Tight. Tight as a duck's arse!'

The laughter continued for some time before Bill trotted out 'and that's water tight.' Helpless and giddy with glee, our shrieks and whoops cut through the still, dry air for what seemed like minutes, only subsiding with the onset of Joe's bout of hiccups as he struggled to catch breath.

'You'd better not say that in front of your mam. That's swearing that is' observed Jesse, at last.

'Well. Our Dad says it sometimes. I've heard him,' I replied.

Bill drew his breath and imitated a deep, manly voice 'and that's water tight.'

Joe shuddered and coughed 'Stop making me laugh. Stop...hic....Talk about....hic....something else.'

I felt my body relax as the giggles subsided and we lay, face up, looking up into the branches of the huge tree.

I offered a diversion, 'It's been ages since we went nesting, innit? Are there any in this tree?'

Joe sat up and stretched his neck and shoulders into several improbable positions until he was finished, 'Can't see for the sun in the branches, but I don't think there are any up there.'

'Got any marbles with you, then?' I continued.

I remember that the four of us then squatted in a circle under that old tree and emptied our pockets. Bill turned up the remainder of his birthday coins and a steel ball bearing. Joe had two Capstan cigarette cards: one showing an Irish setter dog and the other a portrait of George Camsell. Jesse had a small green apple, while I offloaded a tiny red tin soldier whose bayonet had been slowly creating a small hole at the very bottom of my pocket. We piled up the booty at our feet, and resumed lying on our backs, staring up into the tree as the mid day sun scattered spots of light through its branches.

'We could go netting some tiddlers again, down the Bottoms,' I suggested.

Joe brightened to the idea, 'Yeah. We could get the net.'

Bill gave a sigh and scratched at his knees, 'Let's wait a bit. I'm still sweating and it's too hot for the bank.'

Jesse had been quiet for a few minutes, but took up the general theme, 'You know those big white houses on the bank?'

Three voices replied in unison 'Yeah?'

'Those ones they were finishing off, that day when..'

'Yeah' we repeated.

'When our Bill got us into trouble with me mam and dad,' I interjected, receiving a kick from my brother.

'Well' Jesse went on 'they're full up now. All of them. I walked past there the other day on my own and I could see they were all full up with new folks. And they've started making gardens and putting things in them, like grass and flowers and paths and gates, and new trees at the front.'

I sat up again, 'Did you go right up, Jesse? Did you? Did you see the folks, then? Through the windows? Or were they in their gardens? What they like? Like us? Have they got kids like us?'

'Don't be daft, our Tommy.'

Joe now sat up, his hiccups gone, and dipped his hand into the pile of booty at our feet, drawing out the cigarette card portrait of George Camsell and the Irish setter.

'Posh folks like him live in them white houses. With big dogs like this,' he waved the cards under my nose and began barking and howling like a wolf.

I resumed my position and peered up through the tree branches once more, 'You go on your own, Jesse?'

'Free country,' he replied.

'Did you see any of them. The folks what live there?'

'I told you. I saw the gardens and all that. I could see a lady looking out of one of the windows, holding a baby in her arms, she was. It was all done up in white things. The baby I mean. She didn't come out or anything. Just looked out. A way off, she was. The garden was long. It looked nice. Not noisy.'

We were silent for a few moments as we pondered upon life in the white houses on the bank.

'Did you go in?' asked Bill.

'Course he didn't. They might have had guns and things. Like on a farm' I protested, picking up the tin soldier and holding up to my nose to examine his bayonet before placing him back on the ground next to Bill's steel ball bearing.

'How quiet was it, then?' enquired Joe.

Still lying on his back, Jesse held his arm up and spread the fingers of his right hand as far as he could to shield his eyes from the dancing sunlight as it continued to pierce the branches of the horse chestnut with darting rays.

'What do you mean?'

'Bet it's not like our house,' observed Joe 'Specially not when we're all in it. Like at tea time and when we're all going to bed.'

I smiled, 'Ours is not as noisy as yours, but when my dad gets going sometimes… Must be good mind, having a big house and all that.'

'Not having to share a bed and all that stuff' added Joe.

'Good job we don't have as many as you, cos our Tommy's bad enough. And he stinks the place out sometimes'

I rolled over and clambered on top of my brother, my knees pinning down his shoulders as I flayed my arms about above him, fists clenched.

'What you say, mister? Who stinks? Who stinks?'

Tears of laughter mingled with the hot sweat on Bill's cheeks as he shrieked to the others, 'Stinks the place out, he does.'

Finally, the hysteria subsided until, with a single movement, I was ignominiously shrugged off and the four of us resumed our original horizontal positions.

This time, it was Jesse who returned to the theme.

'Anyway, what's wrong with your house. It's a good house yours is. So is yours, Joe. Nothing wrong with them.'

'What if more and more and more and more houses get put up. Like them down Mill Lane and off there. What then? Will ours still be there? And Joe's and yours? What'll happen then? Will they stay or will they knock 'em down and build some more new ones? What would they do with us, then?' I could feel my voice rising as I warmed to this alarming subject.

'Don't be daft, Tommy' replied Jesse, in that easy way of his, the clear blue eyes flashing now, 'Your mam and dad'll take care of you. Like they always have. Nobody's going to pull your house down. We'll still be here. And even if they did, we'll be here still, somewhere around here. All of us, don't you worry about that.'

Joe slowly rose to his feet and walked towards the tree trunk, still looking up into the branches. 'I thought there a nest in here somewhere.'

We trusted him to know about such matters, as it was usually Joe who led the nesting expeditions around the village, climbing the trees and crawling into bushes to examine the wildlife. He had managed to accumulate a wide collection of eggs, which he kept hidden in a wooden box, under straw, in the far corner of the yard at Glebe Farm in Chapel Road, close to where we had laboured on the small patch of wasteland behind the churchyard. The farm was owned by the Dixon family who owned fields behind St Cuthbert's Church and alongside the Bottoms as far as Sandy Lane, and was the main source of milk for many years. Ralph, one of the Dixon boys, had made a deal with Joe to take care of the eggs and keep them safe, if Joe promised to help out in the fields where his father Tom had been a champion ploughman of England, especially at potato picking time or when harvesting season arrived. It struck me that the deal was not an arrangement with which Joe was completely content, as the idea of raiding nests did not sit comfortably with his gentle nature, and Jesse was never slow to test his conscience.

'Haven't you got enough eggs yet Joe?' he asked. 'How would you like it if someone raided your house and took it away?'

Joe shrugged his shoulders and rejoined the group, 'I was only looking. Anyway, there's nothing there. No nests.'

Something in Jesse's gentle chiding struck a cord and I couldn't let it go, 'Yeah. You wouldn't like it. It's like what I was saying. If they build more and more and more and more and more houses, and if we have to find a new one 'cos they've gone and knocked ours down and that and we have no home...'

'Which won't happen' interrupted Jesse.

'Yeah. Which won't happen,' I went on, 'But if it did. Then we'd have to find somewhere else.'

We went into one of our silences again until Joe remarked, 'Well, we could build a tree house. Get some wood. Some planks. And some big nails and some screws and our dads could build it. I read it in some book at school. Folks living in a tree house. We could build it here. Up there in that big conker tree.'

'Yeah.'

'Yeah'

'Yeah we could.'

Fletcher's van puttered its way around the green to the grocers shop, but failed to attract the usual attention which we afforded to it, and so the conversation continued.

'Must be horrible, mind, not having a real house to live in' I said, gratified to see the nodding heads of agreement.

'I mean, a tree house would be alright in the summer when it's like this, but we'd all freeze in the cold weather. And when the snow came. And then we'd have to get down every time we wanted to go somewhere. And our mam wouldn't like that. And our dad would be smoking his pipe up there and she wouldn't like that either and..'

'Tommy!'

Bill's raised voice was sufficient signal that I had overstated my argument.

It was then that the mood changed.

Jesse quietly gathered up the booty and handed back the various items to their respective owners, took a small bite of his apple and then offered a similar bite of the remainder to each of us in turn.

'What do you think that feller's doing? The one down by the old mill.'

His question was met with bowed, silent heads.

Jesse persevered, 'I wonder if he's still down there, sleeping rough.'

The silence which followed was broken only by the noise of the Fletcher boys loading up the van for its next trip.

'Maybe he's built himself a tree house' ventured Joe, at last.

'Not down there. Doubt if he could build it down there. Not enough wood and trees and that. Not on his own' said Jesse.

I remember my feelings of nervous foreboding and apprehension at the idea of another close encounter with the strange man and his terrible scars, as I determined to avail my friends of any notion of a further visit to the mill, at least not today.

'Nobody's seen him about have they? If they had, someone would have said by now. Maybe he's moved on. Got a job. Gone back to Whitby or something' I suggested.

My brother nodded slowly, 'Or he could be down there still.'

'Be cold at night, eh?' Joe remarked, looking up again at his imaginary tree house, high in the branches.

'I bet he's still there. And I bet he's alright. Lighting fires and sheltering in the barn and cooking things. But it'll still be cold on his own' Jesse continued.

'Maybe Cyril and Percy've been down again to see him again' suggested Joe.

We shook our heads in the certainty that this was an unlikely scenario.

I remember so well that conversation, and that particular moment when I decided that it had veered off too far in a direction that was becoming increasingly uncomfortable, and that action was required to recapture the earlier mood. It was a question of seizing the opportunity.

'I'm still thirsty. Why don't we walk over to the shop and get a drink or something?

Come on our Bill, cough up, man.'

To my instant relief, Bill needed little persuasion to hoist himself up from the grass, coins jingling against the ball bearing in his trouser pocket while Joe turned away from the trunk of the tree and started a jerky little dance. Jesse gave a throaty laugh, throwing the remainder of his apple core at the base of the tree where it split into several tiny, white pieces, as he followed us over the green.

Joe made a pledge to us, 'Some day, I will build a tree house, like in the story. But not when it's hot like today. And then when the cold weather comes, and there's plenty of snow on the green again, then we can all build an igloo, like them Eskimos live in at the North Pole. You know, like Miss Bateman told us about that time in class.'

'Like the one we built last year when it snowed. Only bigger eh?'

Bill raised his right arm above his head and brought it slowly down across his forehead and face in a slow deliberate movement to wipe away the damp sweat.

'I wish I was in an igloo now.'

From behind, Jesse's voice reached us,

'Where would you really like to live, though? Hmm? Somewhere high up in the trees or in one of them big white houses on the bank like I was telling you about, with the big gardens and all them big rooms and everything?'

I ventured a suggestion, 'Somewhere that was not too cold, and somewhere not too hot, with somewhere for my things and my own bed and with a window where I could look out of it and see folks and that.'

Jesse continued, 'I bet that fella from Whitby wishes he had somewhere like that an' all. Better than a barn or the open air. I bet if he did, he would get a dog to keep him company.'

My heart sank at the mention of the stranger, but I was reassured by the sense of frustration in Bill's voice as he chided Jesse,

'How do you know he would get a dog? He might not want any body else near 'im. Probably wants to be left alone.'

'Doubt that' replied Jesse. 'You saw how he was with Skip. He had a way with him. He was kind. I don't think he would want to be on his own. Not all the time.'

'Yeah, I suppose' said Joe.

Bill was not to be so easily deflated, 'But he's still a bit, you know.'

'What?' asked Jesse, who had caught up with us.

'Well, I mean. His face and that' said Bill, as he left us to go inside the door of Fletcher's shop. After a minute or so, he emerged with a large orange.

'Here, we can share this.'

Bill dug his thumbs into the skin of the orange to peel it way and carefully separated the segments as we wandered over to a favoured spot near the Salutation Inn, close to where we had first noticed the scarred stranger as he sheltered in the lych gate of the church.

Despite our clear reluctance to return to delicate issue of the stranger, Jesse was in no mood to let the subject drop.

'We should maybe try to help him out. After all, he helped us with Skip.'

The orange had a sharp tang as its juice burst against the dry roof of my mouth.

'What do you mean, Jesse?'

'Well, maybe he hasn't got a job yet. Down at the factory. Maybe hasn't got any money. We could help him find somewhere better to stay. A bit warmer at night.

Somewhere.'

'Why should we?'

'Like I said. When we were looking for Skip the other day and Cyril and Percy were getting all het up and crying. Well, we might have lost him and had to keep searching around all night, but he was there. Skip wasn't scared of him was he? Just went up to him and let him stroke him and hold him.'

Joe was nodding furiously, 'Yeah, and them little dogs, they don't go to anybody if there's something…you know…something not right, or if they think there's danger and that. He wouldn't have gone near the feller, he'd have barked and created.'

Grudgingly, I had to bow to Joe's superior knowledge of animals and wildlife, though the heavy, sagging feelings of apprehension at the thought of another encounter with the stranger down at the old mill, would not leave me.

Bill swallowed the last of the orange segments and spat out a pip from the side of his mouth, 'Just because he looks horrible, with his face and everything, don't mean he isn't…you know.'

'Isn't what?' I enquired.

'Like the rest of us' said Jesse 'and he might need a hand. Might need stuff.'

I was becoming increasingly agitated, 'But we haven't got anything, have we. Least nothing he would want. We're just kids. Like our mam says. Only got what we're stood up in.'

The sun continued to blaze down, as a small group of men walked out from the pub and ambled over the road to inspect the latest additions to Charlie Pool's assembly of motorbikes at the front of his garage.

As we crouched together on the grass, I glanced down along my brown legs to my shoes, warming to my theme,

'Look. Look at them shoes. Our mam says she'll be having to take them to Cobbler Harrison soon to get them mended and I'd better take more care of my clothes and things from now on 'cos me and Bill is getting bigger and we're not made of money. So if they've got nowt then we haven't either.'

'Shut up, our Tommy.'

'We haven't either,' I repeated.

It was difficult to see what more I could bring to the argument as I glanced at the faces of my friends, searching for some sense of finality. The men who had gathered at Charlie's garage had, one by one, donned their caps as if to shield their eyes from the bright sunlight to enable closer inspection of the latest collection of vehicles. Occasionally, one of them would sink down on his haunches and stroke a shiny mudguard, before moving on to sit astride the next bike in the row, all against a murmured backdrop of approval from the others.

'I wonder if he's going to buy that one. He must have some money if he can buy that one. Wish we could' said Joe, quietly.

'Let's go over and see what 'appens' I suggested.

As we ambled over the road, the familiar odours of the garage hung lazily in the heavy afternoon heat. Little was being said among the men. From around the corner of Church Row, a tabby cat strolled to the front of the shop, where the smell of oil, polish and chrome were at their strongest, and rubbed herself against the wooden stanchion of the door. She squatted on the ground growling to herself, her tail flicking fiercely as if in temper at the uncomfortable heat. Suddenly, it scuttled away in fright as the engine of a large red motorcycle caught and laboured, faltered and caught again. A large man with dark hair and sallow complexion was sat astride it, sweat rolling down his brow into the lean hollows of his face and neck as he revved up the engine, his head cocked to one side as the men backed off a little. Slowly, he eased off the throttle and allowed the engine to rumble on for a few moments, turned and caught my gaze.

A huge right arm signalled me over towards him and, in seconds, had scooped me up and onto the machine. I felt his breath against my neck, the hot seat leather against my bare legs as the machine slowly trundled away, around the front of Charlie's garage, past the lych gate of the church, up past the row of tiny cottages along Church Row, turning before the entrance to the vicarage, and then back towards the green to its start point among the men who reassembled as we drew to a halt. His arms spread behind me and then closed around my waist to hoist me back onto the pavement where Bill and Joe were shouting and yelling with wild laughter among the smiling men.

'Did you see...did you see?' I roared, twisting the handles of an imaginary engine, delirious with triumph, running in crazy circles between the two of them until the breath wouldn't come any more and I collapsed into Bill's arms.

We found some shade at the side of Charlie's shop and leaned against the wall as the tabby reappeared, rubbing herself against our legs.

'Where's Jesse?' Joe asked in a strange, quiet voice.

A tiny pool of dry Chardonnay clung to the bottom of the large glass in Fiona's right hand, the rim still pressing at her lips as she stared vacantly through the kitchen window. Her thoughts floated around like feathers in the heavy air. Phil had stayed for a sleep-over at a friends house, Daniel was in his room, the house was quiet, the mood relaxed. Daniel seemed brighter. Richard had spent time with him. Roy had a bit of a cold but the people at Airdale said he seemed cheerful enough. The strange old man in the next room had befriended him. Richard had framed Daniel's drawing and hung it on his bedroom wall. The one with the funny looking building. Richard said he shows real promise. Daniel drew some more. The same bloody house. And still, his friend was there. In his head. But he seemed brighter. That was good. Mister Cartner said it was a good sign.

With a monotonous, hypnotic rhythm, a bright yellow water sprinkler fanned a wide cooling spray across the lawn of the Cedars as, beneath a parasol, Richard dozed behind his sunglasses in the warm morning heat. Fiona observed him. His receding hairline was partly hidden by an old blue sun hat, and while the back of his neck was an angry red, a pair of new white shorts emphasised the way his legs had gone a deep tawny brown over the last few weeks. On the patio table, a black mobile phone rested a couple of inches from the empty glass around which the fingers of his right hand were spread. His bare chest rose and fell as if in harmony with the water sprinkler.

A large circle of dampness covered several of the stone flags where a wall basket containing bright red geraniums and some trailing lobelia had recently been watered.

Fiona watched as it slowly contracted and melted away into the heat.

A tiny bird, with a blade of grass in its mouth, landed on a pair of gardening gloves which were lying side by side, palms upwards to the sky, a couple of feet away from Richard's chair. Its darting movements seemed to energise the feathers in her head, spreading them around again in swirling loops. Phil is out, Roy's OK, Cartner seems happy enough. Daniel's in his room. With his friend. The pal with no name. With no shape.

Slowly, she let the wine glass part from her lips, down onto the cool marble work surface where it stayed, resting, within her grasp.

'Who are you? What do you want with my son?' she murmured to herself.

'Are you kind to him? Do you tease him, like the others? No, don't be so bloody stupid Fee, he's the damned reason why Dan *is* being teased......so...are you a boy, or a girl then?...Good at drawing are you?... Is that what you're showing him?...Why don't you show him something else then?....something bloody useful....instead of daft shaped buildings... towers....whatever they are'.

She threw her head back to swig the last dregs of the Chardonnay, and started to chuckle as the tears of helpless frustration welled in her eyes.

'I wish you'd come downstairs with Dan and meet the family, you'd be more than bloody welcome. Come for some lunch, we're all dying to meet you.'

She was saying the words out loud now.

'Yes, come on down!'

Her shoulders were shaking now.

'Better still, why don't I come up there and introduce myself?'

She slid the wine glass along the cool marble top until it came to rest with a loud ching against Phil's Manchester United mug, and tore off a piece of kitchen roll from a wall holder as she headed for the wood panelled floor of the hall towards the staircase, drying her eyes along the way.

Her warm breath, still laden with the scent of the wine, created a light mist on the ceramic name plate on Daniel's bedroom door.

She tapped gently, three times..

'Darling, are you in there, may I come in please?'

Without waiting for an answer, she entered, smiling, and closed the door firmly behind her, 'How's things.'

Daniel was sat at his desk, his tongue sticking out from between his lips as he gingerly placed a small strip of clear tape over the stem of a small flower, ready to fasten to the page of a large exercise book which was spread out in front of him.

Fiona waited until the flower was in place before approach.

'Nature project' he said.

'For school?'

'Yup. Got to have it done for when we go back after the hols.'

A scattering of assorted, leaves, grasses and small flower heads were waiting, on the desk, to be pressed down into the exercise book. She approached quietly behind him, placed both her hands gently onto her son's shoulders and kissed the top of his head, relieved that he failed to flinch or shrug her away.

'Gosh, you've been really working hard on this, haven't you son?'

Daniel reached out for a piece of grass and nodded his agreement.

'So many. Did you get all of these from around here?'

For the first time, he twisted round in his chair and turned to look up at her.

'Don't be daft Mum, our garden doesn't have this sort of stuff, wild grasses and flowers and things. Our garden's all proper plants. You know. That Dad and you buy at the garden centre.'

Fiona forced a severe frown and lifted her right hand from his shoulder to waft it above his head, making his hair stand up for a second.

'I meant *around* here cheeky. In the lanes. The fields.'

A broad grin spread across his young face, the way it always used to, and she found herself swallowing hard to prevent his seeing the small tears forming. The smile stayed for a few more seconds as he closed his eyes and slowly shook his head from side to side in an exaggerated show of exasperation.

'Well where then, clever clogs?'

Daniel's turned back to his work as his tongue made a reappearance while he fiddled with a piece of sticky tape and pressed the grass into the book.

His mother knelt down beside him and waited.

'A few things were from around here. But I got most of the things from when we went on the nature trip.'

'The nature trip, but...I thought...the accident?'

Fiona's thoughts were suddenly racing back to the day of the trip. Of course. How could she have forgotten that detail? When the school had phoned to say that there was nothing to worry about but Daniel had had a little accident and fallen over. He had been winded and out of it for a minute or two but he was OK. They had taken him to casualty but there was absolutely nothing to worry about. He was perfectly fine. Richard and she had not wanted a fuss making. Daniel certainly didn't. Boys will be boys. Climbing trees. Running around everywhere. Accidents were bound to happen.

She remembered the way Daniel had been quiet for few days after that. In fact, he had never really been the same. Yes, she could remember all of it now. The explanations. The boys had been collecting plants and leaves and fishing for tadpoles and whatever else young lads collect. The geography teacher Mister Holmes had said that Daniel and his pals had been grouped together under a tree when Dan had climbed up to a lower branch. Inevitably, he had fallen off. By the time he had rushed over it was all done and dusted, the boys were gathered around as Daniel lay flat on his back, looking flustered and confused, staring up at the sky. It had taken him a good five minutes to recover himself but he was soon back on his feet. The trip to casualty had been nothing more than a precaution.

After all of that, how could she have forgotten that detail? The school bag. When Daniel had come home from casualty in Mister Holmes car, she had put her son in the kitchen and given him some strong sweet tea while she and the teacher went through the events of the day. It was only when he was leaving that he remembered Daniels bag, and went to retrieve it from his car. A four year old blue Renault she recalled. She pictured herself taking it straight upstairs to his bedroom and unzipping it. Yes, of course. The square plastic sandwich box was there, and the chocolate wrapper. Then the brown box. Lying in the bottom of the bag. The leaves and the grasses must have been in there. The same box which was now on the desk in front of her.

How could she had forgotten that?

'Ah. So these were all from the day of the nature trip?' she said slowly, more to herself than to her son.

Daniel gave a slight nod.

'Mmmm….funny old day that was' she went on, still kneeling by his side. She allowed herself a tiny stare into the boys eyes as he concentrated hard on a particularly tricky specimen, then averted her gaze and picked up one of the small flowers and held it between her thumb and forefinger for a few seconds, before placing it down again.

'I expect you can't remember much about it now.'

Daniel shrugged his shoulders and turned over a fresh page of his exercise book.

'Mummy's little soldier.'

That brought the reaction she had been waiting for. His eyes flashed with fury for a second before they focussed on the reassuring, dancing mischief of her trembling lips.

'Mum!' he shouted as her giggles broke out into loud guffaws which he was unable to resist, his eyes huge with the surprise of the immediate comfort her laughter had brought.

When, at last, they were able to bring themselves to a state of reasonable calm, he felt her fingers stroking the back of his neck.

He sat motionless, his mouth formed in a half smile.

'What did you just mean, it was a funny old day, Mum?'

'Well. I think we were all a bit, I don't know, worried one minute, then relieved that you were OK, then, I don't know really, sort of...waiting.'

'Waiting...what for?'

'For things to...go back the way they were.'

'The way they were, Mum?'

His words nudged the conversation in a way that left her uneasy and a little afraid. She wanted to retain the warmth of a few seconds ago, not veer off in again into that empty, strained mood.

'Oh, I don't know really. Just your silly Mum talking.'

His smile broadened a little, encouraging her to try another tack.

'Can you remember much at all? I mean about climbing the tree?'

Daniel put his finger to his nose and pressed it down on it so that the nostrils flared out, as if it were a flower being pressed into his book. It was a habit he had formed as a very small child and Fiona took comfort from it.

'I remember Jason and Paul...and Simon...and I think Gary and Michael Peacock were there as well. We'd been fishing in the beck and then we had a drink. Mister Holmes said we could have a run around as long we remained in sight, so we had a quick game of kick around with Michael's tennis ball. Then we had a look to see what we'd been collecting for the nature project. Jason had some leaves and plants, and other things, more than the rest of us. I didn't think I had that much. Not as much as he had and I didn't want that. Then I saw the tree and thought...well...I thought if I could get some more leaves and whatever. So I just ran to it and climbed up it. Easy. It was easy. I liked it when they were shouting and looking up and I was looking down, Paul shouted up to see if there was a nests in the branches, or some conkers. I remember that 'cos we all started laughing 'cos you don't get conkers in those sort of trees. Not till later in the year you don't get conkers. He's a wally, Mum. Paul's a right wally sometimes. Anyway there wasn't. A bird's nest I mean. I could see there wasn't. But I thought it would look better if I pretended to look hard, as if there might be one up there. So I reached out, and stretched my arm out.

From the corner of her eye, Fiona observed that Daniel was flexing his fingers, but she forced herself not to look at them, afraid that he would be distracted from his story.

'That's when it happened. I slipped on the branch. I nearly managed to stop myself from falling but I just couldn't keep hold. The branch was a bit slippery and it had sharp bits sticking out.

She recalled the red wheels on his palms when the teacher brought him home from casualty.

'Next thing I was flying through the air.'

Fiona held her breath. She wanted to ask questions. Who came to help? Had he felt pain? Anything. Still, she waited.

Daniel sighed. Twice. Then he resumed.

'All I could see was the sky. Blue sky. I couldn't hear anything. Just a loud noise in my ears. Nothing was hurting, but I couldn't move. Just blue sky and the noise. Then there were voices. I could hear them all shouting things. I could hear Michael and Paul shouting. Then I could see them all. Their faces looking down at me. Jason, Gary and then the others. Except for....' His voice trailed away.

'What darling. Except for who?'

'No Mum.'

'I'm sorry. Take your time Dan....Unless....unless you've had enough. Don't feel you..'

Daniel interrupted her 'No Mum, it's not that. You don't understand..'

He paused and Fiona waited once more.

'Except for somebody else. Somebody else was there. Looking down at me. With the others.'

Fiona realised she was still kneeling and her legs were beginning to stiffen up with cramp. She eased her legs out from under and squatted down next to Daniel.

'Mister Holmes, you mean?'

'No. Not Mister Holmes. It was a boy.'

'A boy?' Fiona was pressing him. She eased back.

'You mean one of your classmates?'

'No Mum. Nobody I'd seen before. He was smiling. Just smiling. Not saying anything. Then he was leaning over me. He was whispering in my ear and he was putting his hands on my face and my forehead. Smiling.'

'And you didn't know him at all?'

'No...I'd never seen him before. He looked a bit sort of...... funny. Bit weird really. But he kept touching my head and it was...I dunno...nice...it was making me feel better....I didn't want him to stop 'cos the noise was going away...the ringing in my ears. He kept smiling down and then he spoke.'

Fiona's eyes never left those of her young son.

'He said "How's that feel then? Any better?" and he helped me a bit. Sort of making me sit up. Then he stood up, next to the others. He winked at me. Sort of in the middle of them. When he stood up, I noticed he had those what do you call them things on. He looked funny.'

'What sort of things?'

'You know. Like Dad sometimes wears. Red things. What do you call them again?'

'You mean braces.'

'Yes. Braces. He had braces on. Except they weren't red. They were brown. I remember looking at them as he stood there. But nobody else said anything. They just ignored him. Then I could feel someone running. I could hear them thudding up on the grass. Mister Holmes. It was Mister Holmes. He was freaking out a bit. Told the others to move away. Told me to stay still while he tested my legs and arms and kept on asking me if I was OK. I could see the lad still smiling in his braces. Next to Holmesy. He didn't tell him to go with the others. Nothing. Then, Holmesy, Mister Holmes, he helped me up and we walked a little bit. I looked behind and the lad winked again. We walked a bit more. Towards Gary and Michael and the others. I looked around again, but he'd gone. The boy had gone. I couldn't see him.'

Fiona took a deep breath.

'I'd like to meet him. To thank him. You haven't seen him since?'

The stem of a small flower twirled around, spinning, between the thumb and forefinger of Daniels right hand. He was staring beyond it, to a place, somewhere, that his mother could not reach. Slowly, his head turned to the brightness of the bedroom window, then to his framed drawing of the curious looking building on the wall, and back again. Then he nodded.

Fiona sighed and shifted her body, now aching with stiffness from the squat position, so that she could rest her chin onto her knees. Without a word, she reached out and squeezed his hand, feeling the petals of the tiny flower flatten between their palms.

Now she could begin to understood.

They stayed that way for several minutes until, finally, she asked

'Is he here now, Daniel? In the room? You can tell me darling'

He brought his hand away from hers, and shook his head fiercely.

'No. Maybe later.'

A stab of pain shot through her legs as she forced herself up from the carpet. She drew in her breath between her teeth and bent her face down towards his to kiss him. Then she turned and left him to his work.

Back in the kitchen, she ran the tap until the water was cold and poured a long glass.

The sharpness of the cool water seemed to momentarily drown her senses, but from somewhere the sound of a mobile phone cut through.

Richard stirred from his slumbers and she watched as he leaned forward onto the patio table, then stood up to listen intently to the caller.

When he entered the kitchen, his face was grey.

'Fee...it's the home. Dad. They've phoned to say...well. They want us to go now. Straight away.'

'I'm afraid I can't let you into Roy's room until the doctor has finished. Shouldn't be too long, he arrived a few moments ago. I'm so sorry. Would you like a cup of tea?'

Richard nodded at the small woman in the blue uniform, and smiled bleakly. He wondered why his hands felt so cold against the warmth of Fiona's as they sat, side by side, in the tiny library room that few of the residents ever used. His eyes drifted across the shelves and scanned the titles of worn out paperbacks donated by relatives, and the video cases containing musicals of the forties and fifties.

They waited in silence until the assistant manager, on duty for the weekend, returned with a tray supporting two pale yellow mugs, a brown tea pot, blue milk jug and cream sugar bowl.

Placing it carefully on a low side table, she smiled 'Won't be long now.'

Fiona glanced at Richard as tea was poured into the mugs.

'When did it....I mean...when Roy....?' She hesitated as her eyes narrowed on the woman's badge attached to her uniform, 'Barbara?'

'Well. I'm so sorry. I'm afraid while you were on your way over, your Dad died. Very quietly and peacefully in his bed. He seemed fine this morning although he didn't want any breakfast so we let him be and kept popping in to keep an eye on him. He didn't want to get up but he said he felt fine. Just a little tired but OK. Then when one of the staff, Jackie, went in a little later, he was turned on his side in an awkward position. He didn't respond when she tried to prop him up so she called for me. That's when I called the doctor and contacted you. I'm so sorry. The doctor just has to certify....then you can see him, if you wish.'

'Thank you,' Fiona squeezed her husbands hand.

'Poor old Dad' he sighed as they slumped back into silence to sip the tea.

The smile returned to Barbara's small, round face 'It often happens this way. With so many of them. I'll just leave you a moment.'

Within a minute, she returned with a young looking man of Asian origin, dressed casually but smartly in a black, short sleeved shirt and blue denim jeans.

'Hello, I'm Doctor Bhalla. You can see him now. This is the death certificate which you will need. It has the time of death. I'm sorry. The staff here will advise you. Please excuse me. I have some other calls to make.'

He nodded and disappeared down the corridor as Barbara summoned a young assistant with bleached blonde hair.

'He looked so peaceful, your Dad. When I went in to his room. Aw, we'll miss him. He was lovely.'

Barbara folded her arms in front of her uniform.

'Probably, he had a heart attack brought on by a stroke. That's what it seems to have been.....would you like to see him now.'

Fiona felt herself jump slightly as Richard replied 'Yes.'

The unmistakeable smell of death filled the small room as they stood in silence at the foot of Roy's bed, the covers enveloping his body so that only his white face showed, much smaller and more gaunt than it had seemed in life, the mouth fixed shut and eyes slightly open in white bewilderment.

After a few moments, there was a light tap on the door as the blonde girl, Jackie, reappeared.

Richard went to the side of the bed, leaned forward to gently kiss his father's pale forehead, straightened himself and forced a cough. Turning to the girl he murmured,

'We'll need to empty his room.'

'Look, there's no rush. No need to do anything now. We have a waiting list but a few days is fine.'

'There's not really a lot to move' said Fiona, looking around the tiny room.

'When Roy came here, much of the stuff that my husband's mother and Roy had collected over the years, we just got rid of it then. There's only a few things to clear.'

Richard edged away from the bed and glanced around, shrugged his shoulders and walked towards the window, where the curtains had been drawn. He drew them back a couple of inches and peered out into the sunshine. On a small grassed area below the window, a young man wearing a chef's white overall was sat on a plastic chair with his feet propped on an overturned plastic plant pot. A cigarette hung from his lips. A young girl came out of the building and tapped him on the shoulder. There was no reaction. Richard watched for a few seconds, unable to hear their conversation and drew the curtain closed again.

'I'll let you know what we arrange' he said.

He glanced quickly around the room again but did not allow his eyes to turn to the bed before following Fiona through the door towards the corridor and the waiting lift. Behind them, they could hear the shrill voice of the Malaysian girl

'Thomas, please. It's alright. Alright. You go back now. Everything OK. Everything OK Thomas.'

When she appeared in the corridor, she was carrying a newspaper in one hand and a glass of water in the other.

'Jackie. Thomas is not calm this morning.'

The blonde girl rested her fingers lightly on her colleagues shoulders

'I'll go in to see him in a minute' she reassured her, 'after I've seen that Mr and Mrs. Latimer have everything they need.'

Fiona pressed the button on the wall to call the lift and turned to her husband

'Oh. I think we've probably done all we can for the moment. Haven't we darling?'

Before Richard could reply, Thomas appeared at the threshold to his room, confused and clearly a little distressed.

'What's happening? Where is he? Where's Roy this morning?' his eyes were wide with anxiety and concern.

Fiona smiled over at him and whispered to the others

'I'll go over and have a little word.'

Richard waited as his wife approached Thomas, reaching out to take both of his hands in hers, talking gently to him, in much the same way as he had witnessed her comforting Philip and Daniel on many occasions. The old man was listening intently, then his head dropped in silent acknowledgement of what was being conveyed to him until, finally, he allowed himself to be led back into his room.

It was not until they were in the car, as Richard fumbled with the Audi's ignition key that she spoke.

'He was so upset. I thought he was going to cry at one point, I really did. Roy and he had become.....well....not exactly big buddies, but.....they used to sit and talk. Remember what that lovely old lady...you know....Mary Thompson....the old Headmistress....remember what she said about him...that he didn't mix with the others. Well, it seems he found a friend in your Dad. Such a shame. I expect he'll probably retreat back into his shell now.'

Richard peered into the car mirror as the car reversed away from a large privet bush.

'Oh and he was telling me that he had enjoyed meeting Daniel, and talking to him about football and other things. I said that we would, maybe, come again with Dan…just pop in some time to keep him company for a little bit.'

Richard cast a disapproving grimace in the direction of his wife.

'Oh I shouldn't worry,' Fiona continued. 'He'll probably forget that soon enough. You know. Old folks don't retain much memory.'

A smile creased her face as she recalled the conversation

'Actually, he managed to make me laugh, old Thomas. He said that the staff all thought he was going bonkers. Then he said that they were right, but he wasn't at the dribbling and drooling stage yet. He still had time left to teach the others a thing or two.'

She chuckled to herself 'I rather like the old chap, and when I said that we might pop back with Thomas, he seemed to really brighten up.'

A greenfinch was preening itself in the warm morning air as it squatted down on the corrugated steel roof sheltering the zinc bath which hung on the wall in the back yard of our house. Twisting its neck around from time to time to straighten the plumage around its neck, it remained oblivious to the background murmurings of domesticity along our little row of terraced houses and cottages. There was a time when the intermittent blasts from the Synthetic factory would have startled it into flight. No longer. Like the rest of us, this tiny creature was adapting to the many sights and sounds which were transforming our village into a small town.

I screwed up my eyes into narrow slits and squinted through the minute gaps between the fingers of my right hand as I tried to observe the bird through the window of our back room, my elbows resting on the solid wooden surface of our breakfast table. The bright glare of the early morning sunshine blazed off the sheet roofing in the yard. I felt my mothers hand gently grasping my wrist, in an effort to distract me. Then she released her grip and got up from her chair at the breakfast table to pull across one of the old curtains.

'Your face will stay like that' she said.

My father's pipe was resting on a shelf by the large kitchen fireplace; a signal of relative calm in the Devlin household, at least for the next hour or so. The last of the breakfast pots had been cleared away, and he would soon recline in his armchair for the first smoke of the day. I cannot recall him ever smoking at the table.

'Did you hear the scavengers last night boys?' he enquired, rising from the table towards the comfort of the armchair.

My mother visibly shuddered.

'Matty. I hate that expression. We've just eaten to boot.'

'What's the scavengers Dad?' I enquired.

He eased himself into the chair and wrapped his large right hand around his pipe.

'The men who come in the night' he replied, the tracing of a smile just visible under his moustache. I looked at Bill for some clue as to the direction this conversation might lead us, but his face remained blank.

'I didn't hear no men' I replied.

'Any,' prompted my mother 'Didn't hear any.'

'Any' I repeated.

His thumb was pressing a large wad of tobacco into the barrel of the pipe.

'Well now. I suppose you wouldn't. Mmmm. But you might have heard their horses.'

Now, I was hooked, and went over to his side, crouching by the armchair.

'Like Tom Mix and the cowboys?'

'Don't be so soft our Tommy. Cowboys round ere?' sneered Bill, without any offer of an alternative explanation.

The smoke was now billowing out from the pipe and slowly expanding in large clouds across the ceiling.

'No son. Not like the cowboys. The horses belong to the scavengers. The men who come to clean out the lavvy in the yard. They come with their horses pulling carts to the houses to clear away what folks have left there, in the closet lavvies. Through the night they come. Council pays them, so it does. In their getups. When no one can see. Come to take it all away.'

My mother rested her arms on the back of a kitchen chair and looked at Bill and I in turn.

'Now that's an end to that thank you. And what are you two going to be doing with yourselves today then?'

We gave each other a quizzical glance and shrugged shoulders in unison. We had not seen Jesse for a couple of days and, somehow without him, the days seemed longer with less purpose.

'Well you won't be kicking your heels around this house on a fine day like this, I can tell you. Your father and I are going to Stockton and we won't be back until this evening. So amuse yourselves but stay away from the house. I've left you some money to go to Lancasters, so you shouldn't go hungry. And don't be going anywhere near the church either. Not today. Tommy Corner has all the choir boys in there today for practice for the big day on Sunday when they induct the new vicar.'

My eyes returned to the greenfinch in anticipation of what was to come next. Mother was in full flow.

'More's the pity that the two of you won't be there. With Guy Henderson and the others, making your mother proud, in your surplices. They'll all be on parade on Sunday. How I've wished to see you that way. Even young Joey, one of your best pals, even him, he was a probationer just like the rest of them. Now look at him. Even Joe's in the choir and I dare say his brothers will be following him. Singing their little heads off with

Tommy Corner they'll be today, while you two are at the Bottoms, Three Corners, or running around the green and goodness knows where else.'

My father gave a sigh and I sensed that his fingers would be starting to grip on the barrel of his pipe.

'It's a disappointment for me, that's all I want to say. With the new vicar coming and everything, for you two sons of mine not to be in the choir on a day like this coming up. Such a day. They'll all be there. Miss Margetts was telling me that the Bishop himself will be coming to induct the new priest. Imagine that. The Bishop of Durham, and maybe the Rural Dean she said. He might be coming. Then there's the others. The whatsits. The canon and the big noises. It's going to be lovely.'

Something in that impassioned speech made me look away from the window. Canon? Big noises? What was that? Mother drove home her main point.

'And after all the time I've taken with you two. The trouble of getting the two of you up and dressed of a Sunday morning, hoping you'd show willing with your pals. Probationers they were. But not you. Now look at them in their lovely surpluses they'll be...'

The sharp sound of my father's pipe tapping three times against the side of the fireplace brought silence to the room.

'Agnes' was all he needed to say to bring things the interlude to a close.

'You're good boys.' His eyes were dancing as he smiled down at Bill and I.

'Run along with you now, and don't be getting yourselves in trouble or we'll be having that lady worker back at our door.'

My mother kissed the top of my head and held me close to her for just a second, then repeated the gesture with Bill.

We washed our hands under the cold tap in the back kitchen and walked out into the yard to consider our plans for the day. No Joe, no sign of Jesse; the day suddenly seemed to stretch ahead as more of a challenge than a joy. The greenfinch cocked its head to one side and flew off.

By the time we reached the Green, the village seemed to be humming like a wasps nest. Fletcher's van was being loaded up; Charlie Pool was suspending a new bicycle from the ceiling of his shop to display in the front window where a couple of men were observing his progress; people were going in and out of the shops and then stopping to talk, perhaps a little longer than was the custom. A smart little black car turned the corner past Church End House, past Poole's and into Church Row towards the vicarage.

Bill and I shuffled along past the centre cottages on the Green until we came to the black mounting stone outside the cobblers shop. These premises had always been the blacksmiths for as long as folks could remember but now they were being put to new use. Old Bob Danby, the previous shoe repairer who lived in West Row close to the Salutation Inn, had retired.

I surveyed the sign from my lofty position on the mounting stone

H.E. HARRISON, High Class Boot Repairer, Only Best Material Used, Workmanship Guaranteed, Hand sewn work a speciality, Parcel Agent for Express & Blumers Motors, Our Motto – Satisfied Customers.

A tall lady, carrying a brown paper parcel, swept past us into the shop, leaving a sickly sweet smell behind her. I peered into a small square window and could make out Mr Harrison, in his ankle length white overall and large cloth cap, examining the leather ankle boots which the lady had just presented to him. One of his legs seemed to be positioned at an odd angle. Suddenly, he took a long, sharp looking, hooked metal gadget from his workbench and placed it against his leg with his left hand. With the other hand he took up his hammer and drove the gadget into his leg. My head jerked back, recoiling in shock and I saw the lady quickly place her right arm against her chest, seemingly in a moment of fright. Then, calmly, he stood up and limped slightly across the tiny shop to write a note which he placed on a small table in the corner. Then he touched the peak of his cap and the lady gave him a small nod in return before leaving the shop. Sometimes, I can still recall the strange blend of leather and dusty paper mingling with her fragrance as she went on her way.

Bill and I watched her for a few moments before the Cobbler appeared in the doorway. His features seemed, at first, a little harsh and rugged but they soon gave way to a reassuring smile. I tried not to look down at his leg but the temptation was too great and it was with a curious feeling of relief and mirth that I glimpsed the shape of his shod wooden leg, poking out from the bottom of his long white overall.

'Planning to stay on that step all day are you?' he enquired.

I jumped off and looked at Bill.

Mr Harrison glanced around him, the smile never leaving his face.

'Another lovely morning' he said, doffing his cap to a couple of passing women.

'Don't you get hot in your cap, Mister Harrison?' I enquired. Bill gave me shove, making me stumble against the mounting stone.

The Cobbler laughed and I felt a strong draught around my neck as he wafted it above my head in mock anger.

'You cheeky little monkey' he roared.

We laughed together for a few seconds.

'Who was that lady came in with them boots?'

He replaced his cap and placed his hands on his hips.

'Well now, here's an inquisitive little mind. I could make use of a lad like you when you grow a bit bigger. That lady was sent from the folks in the Hall, by the station there.'

My father had, on occasion, taken Bill and I down the long walk to the station to see the trains, and I could recall seeing the tower of the old Victorian mansion behind the trees from the road, and the quaint looking lodge at the entrance to the driveway.

He went on 'Seems every body is getting themselves decked up proper smart, Sunday best like, for the new priest coming.'

I pondered on this thought for a moment.

'Aye, you're right Mister, they are' I agreed 'and our Mam says when he comes they're goin' to be a canon and some big noises!'

I could still hear Mr Harrison's laughter from the other side of the road as Bill and I chose a spot under the large tree next to the school railings, to review our strategy for the day ahead.

My brother's question caught me by surprise

'Where do you think Jesse's got to ?'

It was not his way to solicit my opinion in this manner; the usual protocol was to offer a few suggestions and then wait to see if I agreed or disagreed, all the time feigning disinterest. This approach was different and it worried me because I knew that, at its root, was a nagging concern about the welfare of our friend.

'I dunno. One minute we were all leaping about after that man gave me the ride on his motorbike...next minute he's gone. Maybe he knows somethin'

'What about?'

'The canon. The big gun that's goin to be fired, the big noises and that.......what our mam said. Maybe he knows where it is and he daren't let on. Jesse knows about stuff like that. I bet he knows all about it.'

There was a pause while I waited for Bill's response. None came. No giggling. No rebuke. Not even the slightest mockery. Instead, I had been given silent permission to develop my argument.

'I'd love to see it wouldn't you our Bill?' I continued 'I bet its big and hidden somewhere just ready to be wheeled out in front of everybody. Must be somewhere not too far away. Maybe them lads in the church choir know something as well. Joey and the others. Maybe lots of folks know where its going to be fired. What do you think our Bill?'

'If them folks know about it…well, Jesse would have told us Tommy. We're his pals. He would have told us.'

'What if he found out the secret and then someone knew he knew and they captured him somewhere so that he couldn't tell anybody.'

Bill turned his face to mine and simply shook his head slowly. Not enough to constitute outright mockery but sufficient to discourage any further pursuit of that particular line of argument.

Bill sighed and then offered a suggestion.

'Look. If it's something to do with the church choir and all that, then the canon must be somewhere near the church. That'll be why they're all over the place. Practisin' and all that. We could always spy about the place and see if we could find out where it is around there.'

'You mean go round the church yard, lookin?'

'As long as we're careful and quiet. No harm eh?'

'But our Mam said' I protested.

'I know, but what about Jesse? You want to know where he's got to don't you? Better than moping about here all day.'

I pondered on the proposal. It was clear that without Jesse, our little band of brothers was drifting like a rudderless ship. Somehow, he seemed to be the glue which fixed us all together; not exactly leading us but always there - behind us, alongside us, saying the things which got us moving. I never knew what he was going to say or do; I only understood that he made our small world seem much bigger, feel much more important; and it was a good feeling. On that strange Summer morning, I missed that feeling. I wanted it back.

I trailed Bill along Church Row, keeping to the shade of a high wall adjacent to the impressive old church building, away from the row of sun drenched cottages on the other side of the narrow little lane. The shiny little black car, which we had seen earlier, was still parked close to the entrance to the vicarage. Just before the entrance, a set of steep, narrow steps which can rarely have seen the sun, formed a tiny cut in the high wall and allowed access to a 'vicars trod' around the old Saxon tower. We had never taken notice of it before that morning.

Bill whispered 'This must be the way that the priest comes from his house to get to the church door to save him goin' right round and through the gate at the front. Let's go.'

I nodded my agreement and followed behind my brother until we reached the angle of the corner of the tower; from there we could see that we were at the highest point in the churchyard and could look out over the rows of graves and headstones, over the Bottoms to the rim of the valley at the other side of Billingham Beck, towards Norton. There were no words between us as we surveyed the scene for a few lingering moments, distracted from our immediate task by the dramatic impact of a vista which looked and felt very familiar but had never before been revealed to our young eyes from this high viewing point. The fields in the distance were known to us, as were the dwellings in the middle distance and on the fringes, but we had never seen them this way. We recognised a few figures, way off, who were tending a grave; but could not make out any new housing, or new factories. Just the Bottoms as they had been for centuries.

'Hey up!' a voice exclaimed from somewhere to the right, familiar yet strained.

Crouching together at the foot of the church tower, Bill and I peered around in a vain attempt to identify the caller who would, doubtless, undo our bold scheme and condemn us to the wrath of our parents.

In silence, we considered our inevitable fate.

Finally, concluding that escape and a petulant display of false valour were no longer viable options, I stood up and raised my hands above my head before stepping out into the sunlight. Bill followed suit.

There was no trace of mockery in his voice as Jesse appeared from behind the huge slab of a gravestone, just a few yards away.

'Where you goin' boys?'

My thoughts were a curious mixture of relief, elation and embarrassment as Bill and I lowered our arms.

'How long have you been there, snooping around?' asked Bill, his face flushed and the sweat standing out on his nose and forehead.

'Not long....where you goin?'

My fists were clenched and part of me wanted to yell out across the graveyard so that the folks in Norton could hear me, but the other part

83

persuaded me to bluff things out for a little while; to see if we could recapture the impetus of our original plan without losing too much face.

'We're goin' to see if we can find the canon' I explained.

Jesse looked at the ground, then up to the church tower and then turned his gaze towards us, the clear blue eyes almost dazzling in the clear light of the morning.

'I'll come with you, help you look for whatever it is you're trying to find.'

Bill and I walked over towards our friend with wary steps, partly from a lingering fear of being in a place that we shouldn't have been, but also from a familiar feeling of being slightly out of control. It was a feeling I had missed in the last couple of days, one that I liked, and one that always seemed to follow Jesse around.

We exchanged our usual greeting, each boy thrusting his right clenched fist out in front of him while his friends, in sequence, brushed it with their own.

That ritual out of the way, Jesse placed his hands in his pockets and began walking towards the south side of the church building, where the main entrance porch was located.

'Hey, Jesse!' I called out to him 'Where you goin' now? Me and Bill's not supposed to be anywhere 'round here today. Not with all the hoohah and the choir lads and all that goin' on.'

Jesse turned on his heel. 'Well. If you want to find something like a canon, you're not gonna find it lying around in the church yard are you? Nobody would do that. Just leave it lying around in the open. If it's for the big choir thing then it's gonna be in the church isn't it? Somewhere. Anyway, we're not goin' to do any harm. Just taking a look. In and out.'

The sound of the church organ became clearer as we approached the porch way entrance; I didn't like the sound of Jesse's idea but had to concede to the logic which lay behind it; and Bill's vacant expression failed to produce any counter arguments.

An invisible cloud of cool air seemed to envelope us, creating tiny goose pimples which seemed to spread up from my fingers to my shoulders as the three of us crouched against the ancient wooden door. Jesse held the large brass handle in both hands and slowly turned it before nudging the door, quietly, until it opened; the music of the organ and choristers echoing from the walls within. We edged our way through the dark gap and squatted in the gloom at the back of the church, behind the rows of pews. I remember the sun light streaming through the narrow windows, creating white shafts of brightness which bounced off the tops of the pews, harsh against the dimness of the rest of the building; wishing I was out there in the warmth, on the green, among the trees at the Bottoms. The smells of wax, polish, old wood and cold hard stone were familiar from the many Sunday morning services to which my mother had subjected Bill and I.

As my eyes grew accustomed to the shade, I began to make out the features of familiar faces in the choir stalls at the other end of the church. Occasionally, there would be a pause in the singing, followed by some words of advice from one of the older choristers, then a resumption of the rehearsal. Our confidence grew as it became evident that we were likely to remain undiscovered in our hideaway among the pews...so long as we remained silent and out of sight.

I tapped Jesse on the shoulder, and whispered in his ear
'Can you see it anywhere?'
'What?'
'The canon, what do you think?'

He shrugged and then sat up to peer over the pews towards the north side of the church, then swivelled round to look back at the rear of the building towards the font and the entrance to the tower.

I grasped his shoulder and pulled him back down.
'Someone will see you. Keep down.'

He turned round to face me, smiled and whispered back 'Well how are we goin' to find whatever it is if we stay here? Maybe it's in the tower. Or up by the choir.'

I lingered on that possibility for a few seconds.
'Nah. A gun like that is bound to be heavy. They're gonna keep it near to the door so that they can wheel it out and fire it. Maybe it's at this end.'

Bill intervened 'Or maybe there's no canon at all, and there never was. No big noises, eh our Tommy? Just wasting our time 'ere.'

A broad grin spread over Jesse's face and he nodded over to Bill, without saying a word.

I was about to object to this negativity when the sound of the organ took on a strange, sighing noise before slowly petering out into a sad wail.

A loud, bad tempered voice through the air and seemed to echo from the rafters. It belonged to Mr Corner, the choirmaster.
'How many times!' he boomed. 'And still.....How many times??!'
We peered out from over the pews.

'You there! Go and get it going again. And this time keep it going. I do NOT want this to happen in the middle of the service. Do I make myself clear gentlemen? How many times? How many times'

I could sense in the silence that followed that Bill was trying to stifle a giggle but, just at the moment when I feared that Jesse and I would also succumb to the hilarity of the moment, a small figure emerged from the choir stalls.

Jesse observed 'There's Joey.'

We nodded in silence as our friend descended a couple of small steps and scurried to the rear of the organ, where he appeared to bob up and down like a cork floating on water.

Jesse whispered 'I know what that is, that he's doing there. I've seen it before somewhere. At the smithy at Wolviston. To blow the bellows to make the air go and make the old organ go, that's what Joey's doin.'

'To make the organ go? How does that work?' I enquired eagerly.

Bill gave me a shove 'Shhh! They'll hear you!'

Too late! As we crouched down among the pews, Mr Corner's heavy footsteps approached. When he reached the end of our row, he turned slowly and raised himself to his full height, his left arm making an extravagant beckoning gesture, almost as though he was still conducting the choir with a single arm. Silently, we rose from our discovered shelter.

'Good morning' he said, before turning back to face the approaching choristers,

'Gentlemen, do any of you know our visitors?' We followed the beckoning arm, out into the centre aisle.

I remember looking over towards the assembled group of choir boys and watching their feet shuffling about beneath their surplices, with Joey in the middle of them, his face flushed from his exertions with the bellows. A few expectant faces were turned in his direction, but silence reigned among the boys.

Mr Corner's arms were now folded against his chest and he seemed to be rocking on the balls of his feet, in rhythm to some far off tune beyond our mortal ears. He was about to speak, seemingly to announce our fate, when an intense looking man wearing small round spectacles, and a pale linen jacket over a black shirt and a dog collar, emerged from the door of the vestry close to the tower.

'Something amiss, no problems with the music I hope?' he enquired, his brows closely knitted together in a severe frown.

Mr Corner gave a loud cough and began to wave his arms once more, ushering the choristers back towards the choir stalls.

'Mmmm. Let us proceed gentlemen' he called out as he followed them back up the aisle, content to leave our fate in the hands of the priest.

A few glints of sunlight danced on his rimless spectacles as the priest fiddled about with some books and papers lying on a small table near to the font. It seemed to me that he was, somehow, weighing up the situation in his head before deciding upon a sentence appropriate to our crime of trespass. Our heads jerked back with a start as a large prayer book clattered noisily from the small table onto the hard surface of the stone floor, its pages left splayed out in a clumsy fan at the feet of the priest. He seemed to be strangely oblivious to this distraction, as we edged out of the pew. It was clear that Jesse and Bill shared my eagerness to avail ourselves of this fortunate opportunity to make our escape but, as we edged our way, almost on tiptoes, towards the door, Jesse whispered

'Wait a minute…just wait….wait.'

It was one of those peculiar moments that Bill and I had started to become accustomed to and, of course, it took its usual course where our pal was concerned. It had only been a few minutes ago, though it now seemed like hours, that our world had been exclusively focussed on a glorious mission of adventure in which we were masters of our own destiny; now to make matters worse, Jesse was about to sabotage a glorious opportunity to return to that world. Already, those heady moments of freedom and fun had almost faded away, submerged by this strange, cold new reality. Bill and I stood rooted to the spot, in dumb obedience to Jesse's command, as we watched our friend walk back towards the book that was still lying on the floor. He picked it up with both hands, closed it, and presented it to the priest who took it calmly with a slight nod and replaced it among the pile of similar volumes. Then, he seemed to draw in a deep breath and soon we were being marched out of the church into the sunlight and I suspected, from the stern look of concentration which was now fixed on the face of the priest, that we were about to be led in shame through the village to our respective homes, to face the wrath of our parents.

When we were half way down the churchyard path, he suddenly stopped in his tracks and announced 'Do you like apples, boys?'

This was an unexpected diversion, and I felt a tiny surge of hope course through my body which prompted me to be first with a reply; an eager nod of the head.

'Yes, I rather thought you might……what are your names?'

Bill gave the required details and, once more, we waited.

'Well now. There are a few apple trees in the vicarage garden... hmmm...yes, and I suspect you already know that. Hmmmm? Yes well. They're not ready yet. Apples for picking. But in a while, by the grace of the Good Lord, in next to no time...the fruit will be ready to drop from the trees. Not yet mind you. In the Autumn. Which will be here upon us as soon as you know it.'

Bill and I looked at each other as the priest went on, removing his spectacles from time to time to mop his face with a large white handkerchief.

'Well now. I'm sure that it would be satisfactory if you three boys would visit the vicarage garden, when that time has come, as long as you knock on the door so that people know you are there. No need to steal them. No need to hide away like thieves in the night. Do you understand? No need, boys. You can take back some apples, you see. When they're ready.... ...like this one perhaps.'

His small hands dug deep into the pocket of the linen jacket and, from one of them, produced a small green apple which he held up before us, almost as a magician would, and gave it to Jesse.

'Meanwhile, of course, I expect you will not want to compromise your...I mean...you will not want to....well you will want to stay out of trouble. Away from....from trouble, yes?'

I nodded once more.

His brows had lifted and his thin lips surrendered to a smile, his eyes never leaving ours. Then he assumed a more severe stance, and began to rub his left elbow with his right hand.

'Now, I must go...and so must you. Make sure, boys, that you STAY out of trouble. Now be off with you!'

I felt Jesse's hand resting on my shoulder as we trudged off down the church path towards the green, Bill following behind. When we reached the dark shade and sanctuary of the lych gate, we stopped as Jesse tossed the apple to my brother and signalled to us to sit on the wooden bench seat beneath the canopy. When we looked back along the path, the priest was still at the spot where we had left him. He was shading his eyes with his hands, as if surveying the local scenery, looking all around him, at the grave stones, at the trees, the houses. It was clear that his gaze had settled on our shelter when he began gesticulating and pointing with his right arm, waving us away, out onto the green. We trudged off once more, Bill took a bite from the apple and then I stole a final glance back over my shoulder. As I did so, I saw the priest nod and his arm was waving the handkerchief. I waved back.

Lancasters shop was particularly busy in the middle of the day, and it was early afternoon before we had finished our fish and chip, eaten straight from the newspaper, and had settled ourselves at our favourite spot under the chestnut tree by the old school railings. I remember seeing, for the first time, a long six wheeled lorry chugging by on its way from the station towards the factory, with large white letters emblazoned along its side: SYNTHETIC AMMONIA & NITRATE Ltd with the name ICI Ltd added in two places.

The morning's events had left us strangely becalmed, and I felt the need for an injection of urgency before the afternoon drew further on and our parents returned from their trip to Stockton. For a while, we lay there, watching our tiny world go by, the conversation a little stilted. It was Bill who broached the subject of Jesse's absence during the previous few days.

'So, watcha been doin' the last few days? Have you been with your folks all the time? You been around the farm, have you?'

Jesse fiddled with the laces of his brown shoes.

'I've been around.'

This was becoming a little tedious. I wanted the awkwardness to be over as soon as possible, to lighten the mood and start the day over again. Go to the Bottoms. Maybe go fishing for sticklebacks, kick a ball around. Something.

'Bill and me. We've been doin' all sorts of things, playing games and everything with the others and we found some new dens and stayed up late' I lied.

There was no immediate reaction from Jesse, who simply rolled onto his stomach with his elbows dug into the grass, his chin resting in the palms of his hands, watching the people passing in and out of the village shops.

Exasperated, I reached over to where a small twig had been snapped off from the branches of the old tree, clasped it tightly in my right hand and swiped it across Jesse's upturned backside.

'So where HAVE you been then, clever arse?'

Bill's loud laughter rang out as Jesse rolled over in the grass several times before coming to a gentle halt a few feet away, his face hidden from our view.

I had that familiar feeling of blood coursing through my neck and ears, my heart thumping to the usual rhythm which always accompanied frustration, annoyance and burning curiosity.

My body froze and then tensed itself when Jesse eventually turned his face towards us, a deep frown etched on it which I had never witnessed before, filling me with dread. Was this to be our first fight? Will my pride stand up to the inevitable defeat when Jesse's strength and his fury overcome me? Will Bill just watch my demise from the sidelines or will he try to protect his puny younger brother? Or worse, will he side with Jesse?

I threw the twig towards the trunk of the tree and waited, trembling, for Jesse to hurl himself at me.

The assault never came.

The clarity of those moments remains with me now, with the same intensity as the image of tiny fishes circling a sun sparkled jam jar, just a few weeks earlier.

Jesse's eyes burned blue and fierce as he stood over me, hands on hips, and my tears began.

My lungs felt as though they would burst with the pressure of huge racking sobs as my wet cheeks burned in shame. When the expected blows failed to descend on my wretched, outstretched frame, I gazed upwards through swimming eyes at the sky and the floating features of Jesse's scowling face. Slowly, interminably, the frown started to dissolve and fade into a strange, bland expression, then transformed itself into a generous smile which heralded, finally, the glorious, unfettered roar of our triumphant laughter.

I knew that my defeat had been a hundred times more accomplished and decisive than if I had been beaten black and blue. Jesse had reduced me to a shambling wreck and yet it was relief which had finally overcome humiliation. My pal, our pal, still belonged to Bill and I. We were still together, as one, somehow unbreakable.

When the laughter had subsided, I sat up and rubbed my face with the backs of my hands as Bill made an attractive suggestion.

'What about the Bottoms, eh? Should we have a look down at the three corners? See who's down there? Jesse? Are you comin?'

Jesse's face wore an expression that suggested he had already anticipated the idea, but he made no effort to move.

'Don't you want to know what I've been doin?' he asked, quietly, but with enough conviction to suggest that he knew what our answer would be.

'See that over there?' he continued with a nod in the direction of Charlie's garage'

Bill sat up, 'You mean the bike, out in the front? The new one?'

'Next door. The Tower House.'

Now all three of us were erect and gazing intently at the building.

'I told you before, our Mam and Dad call it the Pinnacle' I reminded him.

'What about it? Looks the same as it always has' observed my brother.

'There's nobody living there at the minute. I could tell the other day when you were on that bike with the fella giving you a ride, Tommy. When you were all whooping and leaping about, I had a look up close at it and all of them windows, all the way up, they were all shut up tight. So I knew.'

'How come you knew?' I asked.

Bill smiled 'Cos if someone had been living there, they would have been open, in the heat. Cos it was red hot. Too hot to have the windows down. That's right isn't it Jesse?'

Jesse gave a quick nod 'So while you lot were all leaping around, I had a look round the back at the door where the little yard is, and it was open. So I had a quick look in the yard. Nobody was there. I could hear all the noise, and the bike going past. I tried the door at the bottom and it opened. Just a bit mind you. It was open and you could tell that nobody was in it. Nobody had been in for a bit. Just empty. I could just tell it was empty.'

I could see from the look on my brothers face that he was intrigued.

'What did you do then?'

Jesse plucked a small blade of grass from the ground and twirled it between his right thumb and forefinger. I had seen him do that before, whenever there was something he was going to say that was going to be tricky for the rest of us to understand.

'Well I started to think.'

'What about?'

'No. Not about what. About who. That man. The one down by the Moon's Mill.'

My heart sank 'You mean the fella with the face?'

Jess went on 'The man sleeping rough by the mill. Him.'

Bill coughed awkwardly 'I'd forgotten about him.'

'Well I slipped out of that back yard and I ran hard down to Mill Lane. Down past the fields. To see if he was still there. I had a look around for a bit before I saw the smoke from his pipe. By the wall of the mill. Where we saw him that time. Still there.'

There were a few moments of silence as Bill and I took all of this on board.

'You want to know what happened next?'

We nodded in unison.

'Well. You'll just have to wait!' he laughed, rolling on to his side.

In a flash, the three of us were rolling in mock battle under the tree as Bill and I attempted to interrogate our pal; our methods switching, inevitably from feigned violence to desperate pleas for information.

When it seemed we had reached a final stalemate, Bill sighed with sad resignation. This, of course, was the signal for Jesse to resume his story.

'Well. I told him about the Tower House and how it was empty and that I could show him, so that he could see it for himself. Then he could camp out there until he found somewhere. For a few days. Nobody would know and he'd be alright. Not cold at night. He wasn't going to do it at first, but then he changed his mind and we went there. Minding our own. We went to the door and he told me to go home and he would be alright and he didn't want to get me into bother and that. So he went in and I went back home.'

'You mean, he went in to live in it for a bit? To camp there?'

'Yep'

Bill pointed at the Pinnacle 'So....that means he might still be up there.'

Roy's coffin was decorated with white lilies and bore a simple message printed on a small card 'Rest in Peace Dad. Love Richard, Fiona, Philip and Daniel.'

The smaller of the two chapels was two thirds full. The Latimers occupied the front row, while Roy's sister and her husband were in the row behind, accompanied by an assortment of nieces and nephews. Friends and former neighbours took up the other seats. Upon entering the building behind the pall bearers, Richard had thought he recognised some of them, together with a few of his father's former work colleagues from years ago.

Fiona had chosen Morning has Broken, and then Abide with Me for the end of the ceremony because of it's association with the Cup Final and the recent memory of Daniel's football conversations with his grandfather. It was not until they filed silently out of the chapel into the courtyard area, that she remembered that Roy had, in reality, not been a soccer fan. At that moment, however, it didn't seem to matter and the tune brought some comfort.

Only Daniel had cried, his narrow shoulders gently heaving as he slumped between his parents who linked arms behind his back, for support. His brother's eyes remained fixed, throughout, on the order of ceremony and the hymn book; not once had he glanced over to the blue curtained pedestal where the coffin rested. Richard had listened intently to the eulogy, delivered by the young curate of the local church at Little Smeaton, and recited in his mind the words which he and Fiona had carefully prepared a couple of days ago. Plenty of reference to his patience, his generous spirit, his family and his love of his dear wife with whom he would now be reunited, his friends over the years, the kind people at Airdale Lodge who had looked after him so well in the final years. All the boxes had been ticked and yet, the thought haunted him that, somehow, he had never managed to understand the true essence of his father's character, let alone reflect it in a few words of testament.

Richard walked out into the pale mid-day light and took a firm grip of the curate's hand, to thank him for his services. Fiona and the boys followed and they lined up in a sad little group to greet the rest of the mourners as they left the chapel. Three wreaths and half a dozen bouquets were arranged in a row along bench seats. These were carefully inspected by everyone before conversation slowly began to emerge from among little break away groups.

Rather than expect people to travel back to the Cedars, Fiona had arranged for a small buffet reception to be provided in a hotel less than half a mile from the Crematorium, and she circulated among the little conversation groups to convey the information to them, while Richard stayed close to the boys. He longed for the relative privacy and relief of the single, remaining cortège car which was parked a few yards away, waiting to convey his family to the hotel.

Fiona recognised the bleached blonde hair of the care assistant from Airdale Lodge, who was stood with her supervisor Barbara at the back of the groups.

'How kind of you to come. I hope you can come back to the Blue Bell for a little while?'

'Actually, no Mrs Latimer. Thank you very much, it's nice of you to ask, but we have to get back to Airdale. We just wanted to pay our respects to Roy. Everyone was fond of him. A nice gentle man' replied Barbara.

'Oh that's a shame, but you'd be most welcome. Richard and I appreciate everything you did for his Dad, but I understand. I don't know how you do it sometimes. I'm not sure I would have the patience to deal with so many old folk. I admire you, I really do.'

'Oh, they're lovely most of them. You get used to dealing with all their little problems, and their funny old ways,' added the blonde. 'Mind you, there's some not as nice as Roy, I have to say.'

'Jackie' interrupted Barbara.

'Well you know how they can be, sometimes. By the way, Mrs Latimer, I thought your two lads did you proud. We were just saying, weren't we Barbara? They were so canny. It's a lot for them to take in at that age. I mean it is for us. I still get really upset when somebody passes away. It's hard. I mean I could really do with a ciggy right now but, well you know what I'm saying don't you? I thought they were both lovely boys.'

Fiona smiled broadly and rejoined Daniel, taking him gently by the hand to lead him over to one of the groups in which Richard was making polite conversation. Philip stood a few feet away but made no attempt to join them. He gazed around at the little assembly of strangers, then at the line of bouquets, then at the no smoking sign fixed discreetly to the end of the wall next to a tall rose bush, before his eyes strayed over to where his mother had been standing with Barbara and Jackie. The older of the two women fumbled in her hand bag and withdrew a set of car keys, whispered a few words to her colleague and tripped off gingerly towards the ladies toilet. Jackie pushed her hands deep into her coat pockets and rocked on her heels for a few seconds, before returning Philip's stare with a broad smile. His head dropped in startled embarrassment as she beckoned him over with a flick of her hair.

Philip shuffled over to her side.

'I expect you'll be glad to get out of here and head back home with your Mam and

Dad, aren't you?' she enquired.

Philip shrugged his shoulders 'Suppose.'

'Well. Soon be over now. Look after your younger brother won't you?'

A brief look of disdain spread, momentarily, over his face.

Jackie laughed quietly and continued.

'Your name's Philip isn't it? Your brother, he's Daniel isn't he?'

'Yup. 'Cept he sometimes gets Dan.'

'Daniel's his proper name though. I like it. It's a nice name for a boy.'

'What's wrong with Philip?'

'Oh nothing. Nothing at all. Two good names.'

There was no sign of Barbara.

'Listen Philip.'

'Phil. I like Phil better.'

'Phil...would you do me a little favour.'

'What is it?'

'Well.....it's nothing really. It's just that. Well, you remember the old gentleman who has the room next to where your Granddad was. Do you remember?'

'No.'

'No?....no it was your brother wasn't it? Daniel. It was Daniel who used to sit with him. Well, it's just that...'

'Why don't you ask Daniel to do you the favour?' replied Phil.

Jackie looked down at her watch and then thrust her hands, once more, into her coat pockets, rocking on her heels again as she did so.

'No, we're going now, me and Barbara. I don't want to disturb your Mam and Dad and young Daniel. I just wondered if you would give them something..'

'What? Give them what?'

'Well it's nothing really? This...it's this,' she drew out a plain, slim white envelope from her coat pocket and passed it to Phil who stared glumly down at it for a few seconds.

'What's this?'

'Probably a sympathy card. It's from the old gentleman I was talking about. The one in the next room. The one who used to talk to your Granddad and your brother. He must have got one of the girls to go the shops to get him a card, so that he could send it this morning. He asked me, this morning, if I would give this to your Mam. Or your Dad. I nearly forgot earlier on, but then I remembered. He seemed a bit agitated about it so I thought I would just, you know....humour him a bit.'

'Humour him? What do you mean?'

She paused. 'Oh. Keep him happy. He's a funny old chap sometimes. Anyway, I said I would. So, if you wouldn't mind just passing it on to your Mam, when you get a minute. There's a good lad.'

Philip was about to ask her if he should open it, when his father's voice called over to him.

'Phil? We're going now. Come on son.'

Carefully, he placed the envelope in the inside pocket of his jacket and smiled up to Jackie.

'OK. I'll give it to them,' he said, as Barbara emerged from the ladies toilet, waving her car keys at her colleague. Then, the two women were gone.

As the black cortège car slowly negotiated its way around the narrow drive leading to the exit of the crematorium, none of the Latimers spoke a word until the vehicle moved out of the gates into the busy dual carriageway.

'Thank you, you guys. It all seemed to go well...you know what I mean,' sighed Richard as he took hold of Fiona's hand and gave it a gentle squeeze.

'Mmm...' she murmured in agreement, 'It was nice that there were quite a few there, I thought. Didn't you? People on holiday still, you know. The Rhodes are still away. Otherwise they would have been there. All of that. But there was quite a good turn out for him....nice that.'

The car picked up a little speed.

Richard looked at his two sons, 'I wasn't expecting to see anyone from Airdale.

Good of them to turn out like that. He would have appreciated that, the old boy.'

He was still gripping Fiona's hand. She squeezed back and he released it.

'Mum,' said Philip, 'One of them, from the home. She asked me to give you something.' He withdrew the envelope from his inside pocket and passed it over to his mother.

Richard's jaw dropped 'Surely it can't be a bloody bill?'

'Darling, don't get excited. It won't be,' she reassured him

Philip's eyes returned to the road outside 'The lady. The blonde woman. She said it was from the old guy in the next room to Granddad Probably a card or something. She asked me to give it to you, cos he wanted you to have it or something,'

For the first time, Daniel sat up straight in his seat, but remained silent.

As the car pulled into the car park of the Blue Bell hotel, Fiona could see that some of the guests had already arrived ahead of them and were making their way, slowly into the front doors.

'Darling, if you want a couple of moments to yourself, wait here in the car. I'd better go ahead through to the back room and see that everything is in hand. I'll take the boys. When you're ready, it's straight through the front doors, head to the left past the main lounge. Here, in case I lose it, I'll give you the card from that old chap. Don't lose it will you?'

She kissed Richard gently on the cheek and dropped the card into his lap, thanked the driver and took the boys into the hotel.

Richard smiled weakly to the driver 'You've been very good. Thank you. Would you just wait a second?' He looked down at the envelope in his lap for a moment and then slid the nail of his right forefinger through the thin paper. There was no sympathy card inside. It took a few seconds for him to register the image, still clear on the old sepia photograph which he was now holding in his right hand. He felt his throat tighten as he recognised the tall, narrow, curious building, pictured in exactly the same proportions that his youngest son had so carefully and skilfully depicted in his much admired drawing. He noticed that a small note remained lodged inside the envelope. Slowly, he withdrew it. It was typed.

Dear Mr and Mrs Latimer. I will miss Roy. He was the only one here I could talk to. I have kept this photograph for years and never shown anyone. Nobody. I would very much like to speak to you both and young Daniel again, if you ever care to visit.

T

To this day, I can't remember climbing the stairs to the top of the Pinnacle, only the long silence as Jesse, Bill and I surveyed the landscape from the heat of that little room at the very top. It was as if we could almost have reached out through the heavy sash window and touched the roofs of the little houses and cottages; could have thrown a ball and watched it land on the green and bounce over the old brewery site; could have picked up old Mister Greenley as he sneaked out of the Salutation and repositioned him in our school yard.

This new perspective transformed all of the old, familiar and critical landmarks of our little world and transformed them into peculiar, awkward shapes; instantly recognisable but now strangely remote and distant. From the ground, the individual chimneys and smoke stacks of the Synthetic factory had seemed close but somehow separate from our village. Here on the horizon, from above the roof tops, they had forged themselves together into a single, cohesive, terrifying army of invaders.

'Best not look out for too long. Don't stay too close to the window in case somebody notices us' advised Jesse. We withdrew a little into the room.

She said it was from the old guy in the next room to Granddad Did you see him, our Bill? Scratching his bum. Thinking nobody was watching him.'

The recollection heralded several long moments of hysterical giggling, before my brother turned to Jesse.

'What do you think then? Has he gone, eh? Do you think that man's gone this time, Jesse?'

We edged a little closer to the window and scanned the view, once more, for a few minutes. My throat was dry with excitement and the heat of the room had brought me out in a sweat, 'I'm going to sit down in this corner, next to these things 'ere.'

The room was bare, not even a piece of carpet on the floor, except for a flat, round tobacco tin and a brown pipe whose stem had snapped and broken off at the end.

Jesse and Bill crouched down beside me.

'Looks deserted, doesn't it?' observed Jesse, running his fingers along the lines of the floorboards.

'Anybody got an apple?' I enquired.

Bill wafted his hand above my damp hair, 'Don't be so soft, man. We'll be gone from here soon enough. We'll get a drink after.'

'Well what *have* you got, then?'

Jesse thrust his hands in his pockets and pulled out the inside linings to reveal a couple of marbles. Nothing more. Bill then removed some coins and a couple of broken biscuits which created a small dusting of crumbs on the bare wooden surface. They turned to me.

'I haven't got anything.'

'You must have something' insisted my brother, 'Let's see, come on.'

'Yep, come on Tommy. I thought we always shared everything. The three of us, and Joey if he was here. We share.'

My hesitation was the signal for Bill to launch another of his regular assaults on my skinny frame, and it only took a few moments before my arms were pinned to the floor and I was looking up at Bill as he straddled my stomach.

'Jesse, have a feel in his pockets. See what's in there, eh? An apple, maybe? Some money and lots of other nice things? Let's have a good look. Go on Jesse!'

I wriggled about in vain, and shrieked a few muted protests. Out of the corner of my eye, I could see Jesse's smiling face, but he made no attempt to search my pockets.

'Tommy's going to show us, himself, aren't you? Let's see. Let him be, Bill.'

My brother gave one final wriggle of his hips, just to let me know that it was *his* decision, and his alone, to decide when I should be released from my current undignified position. In truth, of course, we both knew otherwise. As I was released from Bill's clutches, the old familiar burning blue shone in Jesse's matchless eyes, and we surrendered.

'There's only a couple of things in them. Nothing to eat. No money or anything. Just a couple of things I picked up. Nothing. Honest,' I pleaded.

Jesse reached over into the corner of the room where we were crouched and flicked the broken pipe to one side, then picked up the round tobacco tin. He opened it slowly and held it upside down like a magician performing a trick to demonstrate that it was empty.

'Here,' he suggested 'There's my two marbles. I'll put them in here. Don't bother with your biscuits, Bill. Just put the coins in. Now you, Tommy. Put your stuff in here. Go on.'

I reached into my left pocket and pulled out the empty lining, revealing the large hole at the end of it.

'Whatever was in there, has gone now. You want to ask your mother to fix that, or you'll be losing stuff all over the place,' observed Jesse.

Bill added 'Our Mam does that but I bet he forgets to ask her, don't you our Tommy? Joey's sisters do all that as well. They learn all that at school, you know.'

'I'll ask our Mam, when we get home, I'll ask her,' I muttered.

There was a brief pause in the proceedings.

'What about the other one, then?' demanded Jesse, giving the tobacco tin a rattle, the coins and the marbles creating an echo, off the walls. He placed the tin at my feet, and I fumbled around in the right pocket of my trousers.

'What's that?' asked Bill, as the perfectly round, shining pebble, joined the other offerings in the tin.

My voice was little more than a whisper.

'It's my pebble. From when we were diggin' the ground over by Chapel Road...when our Dad made us go to help Stan Smith and the lads with the diggin'... and we went swimmin' and the Norton boys......'

'I know...I remember. You had a queer do and shot it at the wall, after we had all got it looking good, the ground, all flat and looking right. You mucked it up so Jesse went and straightened it up and that.... I remember.'

I felt Jesse's gaze silently burning away.

Bill continued 'Never mind that, then. Anything else?'

I fumbled deeper into the pocket and withdrew my hand. It hovered over the tin, concealing the contents in its grip until the black jet carving of the horses head dropped, with a light rap.

Bill scratched his nose but said nothing.

'So, you kept it. I'm glad. I was wondering whether you would lose it,' said Jesse, quietly.

Bill reached out his arm, 'Let's have a look at it.' He tossed it about in the palm of his hand and passed it to Jesse, who stroked it for a few seconds between his finger and thumb, polished it against his trousers, and replaced it in the tin.

'I thought you didn't like that fella, our Tommy.'

'I never said that. He gave it to me. So I kept hold of it. He looked after the Atkinsons dog remember...Skip...he was alright. So, when he gave it to me, I kept it.'

He continued, 'What about the pebble? Can't play marbles with it. Why did you keep that?'

I shrugged my shoulders because the truth was that I didn't really understand the compulsion that drove me to keep them close; all I knew was that I didn't want to let them go. Somehow, in a way that I was too young to comprehend, they had become more than mere trinkets, objects that shone for a few days and then faded away with the passing weeks and months until they disappeared, unmissed. No, they were more than that. They were touchstones. Comforters.

'We may as well close the tin. Put the lid on them. You keep them, Tommy. Here.' Jesse placed the lid back on the tin and passed it to Bill, who offered no objections to the proposal and passed it on to me. The thin material of my trousers stretched out in protest as I forced the tin into my right hand trouser pocket.

'And don't forget to ask your Mam about the other pocket.'

Bill's eyes turned to the broken pipe, lying in the corner. He crouched on all fours, picked up the pieces and pretended to smoke from the remains of the barrel.

'This is how our Dad smokes!' he exclaimed, his thumb enveloping the barrel, his lips forced and twisted into a contrived and exaggerated curl, as if blowing smoke through the corner of his mouth.

He snarled 'You'll do what I tell you boy, so you will!'

Jesse and I rolled across the floorboards, laughter ringing around the room.

'Let me have a go! I want to do that. Come on our Bill!'

Bill shoved me away, trying to stifle his giggles as the laughter grew wilder.

Jesse joined in the fun, pushing me aside as he attempted to wrestle the pipe away from my brother until, soon, I couldn't tell which one of them had hold of the thing, as the soft blows reigned down in all directions.

I remember the helpless laughter as I found myself on the bottom of the heap, the breath taken out of me by the pressure of the other two on top as, somehow, I caught a glimpse of Bill's outstretched arm with the pieces of pipe clutched tightly in his grasp. My fingers gripped the sides of his ribs and squeezed, and the reflex reaction was immediate. The pipe fell from his fingers to the floorboards, inches from my nose. For what seemed an eternity, they remained there, with none of us able to free our entangled limbs to claim the prize. Then it was that I felt the pressure relax a little and managed to force my wrist through a gap between Bills leg and the wooden floor. I felt the barrel of the pipe in my fingers and began to wriggle furiously beneath the other two until, finally, a fatigue brought on by laughter and heat, weakened their hold and I was free.

We fell back against the wall in exhaustion and I inspected my trophy, trying to piece together the broken parts of the pipe.

'It's completely busted' I breathed.

Slowly, we seemed to gain our composure. Jesse was the first to stand up, as if signalling that we should be leaving the place. I followed suit, the pieces of pipe still in my right hand, then Bill straightened up and stretched. As he did so, I felt his hand grip my left wrist

'Think you're clever, our Tommy?' he laughed, 'Come on, give us one last puff on the old pipe.'

I remember that we were laughing again. All three of us. Then I remember that Bill stumbled and a piece of the stem of the pipe flew away towards the window on the other side of the room, the side that looked out over the little yard and over to the lych gate and the church. We seemed to career over towards it. We were still laughing. Then as we shoved and pushed, I saw Jesse slipping, and reaching out with his arm as he tumbled. There was a sharp crack as his hand went through the glass, puncturing it with a curious, neat hole; the shattered pieces falling onto the ledge and out into the yard.

The silence that followed stays with me.

Jesse held his hand close to his chest, 'Go on. Go!'

Bill and I looked at his white face, the clear blue eyes now dimming. There was no appearance of shock, or even bewilderment. Just a look which terrified me. A resigned expression. Not of fear, or anger. It was sorrow.

Bill grabbed me by the shoulders and pointed me towards the door leading down to the steps. Just as I could not recall my entrance into the Pinnacle, neither can I recall our departure; only that it was the last time that I ever saw Jesse alive.

As is the case with gentle, courteous men, Henry Cartner often spoke too loudly on the telephone.

'John, let's talk about yesterday's meeting with the Latimers. We've both seen Daniel on a number of occasions now, and his Mum; but it was good to get them together with Dad. When Daniel's mum phoned the other day to make the appointment, I sensed that something had changed, but I wasn't expecting what we heard, were you?....Let's talk. See you in a couple of minutes, then.'

Henry picked at his fingernails for a few moments and then lifted his large head as the pale morning light forced its way through the window blind onto the glass front of the old wooden book case, a few feet from the edge of his desk. His eyes took in a long row of identical blue health authority manuals, then an old Thesaurus, various medical journals, and a large green, leather bound volume which had travelled with him through the years. He tried to recollect the last time that he had opened its pages.

Henry's large hands fidgeted with the bundle of papers and files on his desk, then went to his half rimmed spectacles, which he removed and placed on top of the pile, before rubbing his eyes. His right hand removed the large, floppy handkerchief from the breast pocket of his jacket and he used it to wipe the lenses of his spectacles, which were then returned to the bridge of his nose.

He nad formed an effective, if unconventional, working relationship with John Stockley whom he regarded as a good listener. For his part, Stockley was astute enough to recognise his own value as a sounding board.

He hummed quietly to himself until his colleague arrived and, with a broad smile of welcome but without waiting for him to settle into his seat, began.

'I always felt that Daniel's Dad was, a little, in denial of what was happening with the boy. Not so much through what he said, but what he *didn't* say. What do you think. John?'

Stockley took off his jacket and draped it over the back of his seat

'Well, perhaps your right, she's been to see us far more often than her husband and I don't put that down entirely to his work commitments, though it will have a bearing.

No, I tend to agree, Fiona has been far more forthcoming.'

Henry leaned forward 'About *what,* though?'

'About the imaginary friend. Particularly during the last couple of sessions. Seems she was able to get more from Daniel about this friend......when he first appeared in Daniel's life, and so on.'

'Yes. I can see that. You're referring to the accident on the school trip. We have all of the medical reports and so on. Physically, no problems, but that was clearly the start.'

Henry rapped the desk with his right hand, picked up the telephone and requested a pot of tea.

'Down to business, let's go through the meeting, compare notes and see where we are. Have you had time to compose you thoughts and produce anything?'

'Yes Henry, I've done a first draft of my record of the meeting. We can go through it. I've printed off a couple of copies.'

'Good man. I'm most grateful to you.'

When the tea arrived, both men took a few moments to scan through Stockley's report.

'Talk me through it, John.'

'OK. Well, the start of Daniel's school term is only a week away. They start later than the other schools. He seems fine about it.'

'Nevertheless, do you think he was apprehensive?'

'No, he seemed remarkably relaxed actually.'

'Agreed. His Mum and Dad both supported that view when I asked them. We have the school reports and so on.....'

Stockley turned over a page in his file, 'It was the discussion with Mrs Latimer that was the most notable part of the meeting, and I tried to record exactly what she reported.'

'Yes. Precisely. The father's input as well, of course. Fascinating.'

Stockley inhaled 'Shall I just go through this, line by line....and you can see if I've captured what she said?'

Henry nodded.

'Remember, this is only my first draft.'

Henry smiled and noticed, for the first time, the tiny puncture mark on his colleague's left ear lobe.

'Fine, and I'm grateful. We'll amend and add any additional material when you've gone through it. There may be something you've missed....but let's see, John.'

'Sure. Fiona, Mrs Latimer indicated that something had occurred on the day after her father in law's funeral....that had caused the family much distress.'

Richard and she had both agreed that they wanted to get back to a normal routine as soon as possible, mainly for the boys although both Philip and Daniel had seemed to cope pretty well. Philip had come home and phoned a school pal and gone round to his house, and then he'd phoned to ask whether it was OK to sleep over. Richard had checked that it was alright with the boys parents, confirmed that Phil had his mobile phone and a back door key just in case, and had given his permission.

Daniel had spent part of that evening watching television downstairs and had then gone up to his room to play on his computer. Richard and she had chatted about the forthcoming school term and so on. Both of them had agreed that they would wait for a week or so before they considered what to do about Daniel and the matter of the drawing and so on....'

Henry waved a hand in the air 'Let's just leave the drawing issue for the moment. We'll cover that when we've gone through the review of the events. I just want to make sure that we've got the time line right. Go on John.'

'The following morning had started as a fairly normal day. She remembered rising early and watering the plants on the patio as it looked as though the weather was going to stay dry and everything was parched after the long hot summer. She and Richard had chatted about getting the garden tidied up and ready for the change in the weather. Richard was up early to meet some clients in Stockton and had indicated that he would try to get home early in the evening, but couldn't promise. Daniel had also been an early riser that morning. She explained to the boy that she thought it would do him good to get out of the house for a while and so she offered to take him out for the morning; to the coast or the countryside, the choice was his. He opted for the countryside because Miss Jenkins, at his school, had suggested that the class should read about nature, birds and so on, and should use the summer holidays to enjoy the fresh air and find out a bit more about trees and plants. Daniel showed his mum a book about birds and trees and told Fiona that Miss Jenkins had explained to him about collecting leaves, plants and so on. He had enjoyed the lessons with her, including the nature outing which she had helped to organise...up to the accident, of course. He'd like to do some more, and learn how to take care of animals and wild things so that he could have a dog. She sent him upstairs to put on his trainers, not his shoes, if they were going to be traipsing over the fields. In turn, he asked her to bring a couple of spare freezer bags so that he had something to put all of the leaves and plants.

Fiona was looking forward to spending some time with Daniel and the mood was light.

Then she started to worry about Philip, in case he came home from his friends to an empty house, so she prepared some sandwiches and crisps and left them in the fridge, accompanied by a note with instructions about taking some clothes out of the tumble drier. She also wrote that she expected to be back at the house just after lunch and that he should phone her as soon as he was back at the Cedars.'

Henry observed 'All very mundane so far.'

'Fiona mentioned that Daniel had seemed quiet but fairly cheerful in the car as they made for Yarm. She parked behind the high street near to the supermarket where she bought a French stick, and she and the boy had then walked through the viaduct arches to spend twenty minutes or so by the river bank, where he had collected one or two leaves and placed them in one of the freezer bags. She remembered that she had struggled back across the high street cobbles, still carrying the French stick and keeping an eye on Daniel as the traffic passed by. Once in the car, she phoned home but there was no response. She had not been concerned and assumed that Phil was still at his friend's house. She left a message on the phone for him to take the clothes out of the tumble drier and place them in the basket next to the machine…and that she would be back just after lunch…and to read the note she had left in the fridge by the sandwiches.

Fiona suggested that they visit Preston Park to collect some more grasses, but Daniel felt that he would not be able to collect much more than he already had and he knew where the best stuff might be. She remembers feeling uneasy when he mentioned that he would like to go back to the Billingham Bottoms Countryside Park area to look around the beck.'

Henry removed his spectacles and leaned forward 'Well, I can understand that, of course. It's interesting that while Mrs Latimer was a little perturbed, Daniel had no qualms about returning to the scene of his accident on the school outing.'

'Unless Daniel was, I don't know, maybe trying to overcome his fears by going back to the scene, this time with his Mum for company,' Stockley suggested.

As he relaxed back into his seat, Henry replaced his spectacles and fingered the notes once more, 'But as we now know….in the event, they never made it to the Bottoms.'

'No, that's right. At some point on the journey, Fiona had mentioned that she needed to stop for a coffee. Daniel had groaned and they had both laughed. That had pleased her, and she emphasised the point to us that, at that point, they were both in a relaxed and happy frame of mind, and that she felt that the morning trip was doing Daniel some good.

Then Fiona mentioned that she was unfamiliar with the roads on the north side of the river and had pulled off the A19 at the wrong junction, at Portrack.'

Stockley paused and smiled 'Not the best place to get lost.'

Henry nodded, 'Mmmm. I know it.'

'She found herself coming off too early and so they were heading past the factories, along the road which goes past all of the sheds and chimneys, and so she decided to take the first turning which would take her in the general direction of Billingham. The mood was still very light and she mentioned that she had said to Daniel that it was a sort of mystery tour. He seemed happy about that and even joked that she was the only mum in the world who would take her kid to a factory site to collect plants and leaves. She remembers that they had both laughed about that.

They arrived in the older part of Billingham and she stopped somewhere near a row of shops and pulled in. They found somewhere to have a coffee, Daniel had an orange juice, and they chatted about school, about cars, television programmes, and other small things.

Then she had phoned home again. This time, Philip had answered. They had a brief conversation and he mentioned that had read the note. Mrs Railton, the mother of his pal, had dropped him off and she was still there outside, waiting to make sure he was alright. Fiona asked him to put her on the phone. The two women had a brief conversation and Mrs Railton indicated that it was fine for Phil to come back to her house for a while and she would drop him off, a little later. Fiona reassured them both that she would not be too long.'

Henry interrupted 'Remind me...did she say how Philip reacted to that?'

Stockley did not look up from his notes, 'Only that he had grunted and said that he was a bit bored and was looking forward to going back to school, to see the rest of his pals.'

He continued.

'Fiona and Daniel then headed back towards the car with the intention of driving to the Bottoms, when Daniel said that, before they did so, he wouldn't mind having a quick look around the local area near to the Green.

She mentioned to us that she was a little surprised at this request, because she thought that Daniel would have wanted to hurry down to the beck area at the Bottoms, to collect more specimens. She wondered whether he was a little apprehensive, remembering the accident, but was happy to go along with the idea if it kept him happy and relaxed.

They spent the next five minutes or so meandering around the shops and houses around the Green, and she remembers making a remark to Daniel that it was a bit of a quiet, boring backwater....and he had asked her to explain the meaning of the word *backwater* .

t was then that she first referred to a change in Daniel's mood: he became quiet and the conversation almost dried up as he appeared to drag his heels behind her. She wondered if he was getting tired, or a bit bored, and she remembered trying to gee him up a bit by pointing out one or two of the more interesting landmarks such as the old church, and so on. Daniel, however, seemed to retreat.'

There was a small silence as Stockley recalled that it had been at this point of the meeting that Fiona Latimer had been close to tears and had stopped to compose herself. He had fetched her a chilled drink from the water cooler, and her lipstick had left a deep red stain on the rim of the plastic beaker.

Henry waited.

'Fiona noticed that Daniel was very pale and wore the expression that he always had whenever his "problems" rose to the surface. She asked him if he was alright and whether he wanted to go to the Bottoms or back home, but he simply shook his head and took her hand. This was a little unusual, as he had not held her hand for a long time and she had assumed that he had grown out of the custom. They walked aimlessly for a while, slowly past some shops towards a small grassed area, across which she could plainly see an old wooden structure, a canopy leading to the church yard.'

'That would be a lych gate,' said Henry.

'It was at this point that Daniel became agitated. She said.......he was looking over the grass as if searching for something. Tugging at her hand. Tears in his eyes. She was begging him to tell her what was wrong, but he was simply shaking his head in distress.'

Henry held up an arm, paused, and then waved his hand to signal that his colleague should continue.

'Fiona crouched down and held him close to her, then asked him if the churchyard reminded him of his grandfather's funeral. Daniel shook his head again and began sobbing, finally screaming in anguish. He was in so much distress that she gave up trying to extract an explanation from him and can't remember how she got them both back to the car. They sat in it for a quarter of an hour or so, while he calmed down. Then she drove them both home. Back at the Cedars, she opened a tin of vegetable soup and they stayed in the kitchen, neither of them saying much until Philip arrived back home.'

Henry whistled through his teeth 'Quite an unusual little drama, John. When I asked Mrs Latimer if she had subsequently discussed the incident with Daniel, she said something interesting to me. Apparently, when Daniel had eventually calmed down, she had asked him if he wanted to talk to her about what had happened. Daniel was very reluctant to do so, and sat on the edge of his bed looking very glum...but no longer hysterical. She held his hand until, finally, he told her that he couldn't talk about any of it, because it made him too sad. He didn't know why...only that the place which they had visited in Billingham, near to the church, had made him feel sad and frightened. Frightened, because he had never felt so sad before...not even when his grandfather had died. He didn't like the feeling.'

Stockley nodded 'That was born out in the session we had with the boy.'

Henry continued 'If we accept the narrative that you've outlined in your synopsis, the time line and so on...and I have no reason to disagree with the sequence of events as you recorded them, John,.....and we put them together with the input from Richard...'

'You mean, his description of what happened on the day of his father's funeral, Daniel's drawing and the old sepia photograph of the odd-looking building?'

'Exactly. Put them together and there is thread. Something about those images...in the boy's head....how on earth did they get there? Why are they there? Who or what put them there?'

Stockley pondered for a moment 'A picture book that he has seen, perhaps? Are you suggesting that Daniel might be autistic in some way? A savant? Like Stephen Wiltshire? Part of the brain working in a pure, mechanical sort of way, able to record with photographic precision what the eye has merely glimpsed in a few moments.'

Henry waved his large hands in front of his face.

'John, John.....too fast, too fast...'

Stockley took a deep breath 'There's an image, yes? An image that managed to penetrate his mind, almost unnoticed, so that he can't recollect where he discovered it?'

'Precisely. In the case of someone like Stephen Wiltshire, an extremely rare case I might add, it is much different. He is able to observe consciously, not subconsciously, a building or object for a few minutes and then recapture it in every detail at a later time. This is altogether different, John.'

Stockley was silent for a few moments 'Then what is the mechanism, the trigger, that provided the impulse to recreate that old sepia photograph in a drawing. When did it provide the spark in Daniel's brain? Maybe at school, while he was emotionally upset by his school pals? Maybe there's some sort of strange association between the image of that building and something unpleasant that he's experienced and he's blotted....'

Henry's arm was raised once more 'Let's not get too far ahead of ourselves, here.

What about the parents? How do you think they are handling this, John?'

Stockley gave a slight shrug of the shoulders 'Well, all things being equal....'

Henry cleared his throat 'There are no magic formulae for bringing up children, John. No secrets to being a good parent. How the Latimers are with their children must come out of what...who...they are. Do you see what I mean? Look... true vexation with a child is much preferable to false forbearance, because the child knows that it is his parent that he is dealing with, not some unreal façade. Kids depend on it for growth: that real human interchange. Parents want to be perfect. Impossible, thank God. Nevertheless, being conscious of their imperfections makes parents uneasy, because they feel they fall short of their ideal. And because they are not ideal, they start to think they are no good at all. I would rather that parents like the Fiona and Richard Latimer simply do their best to be *good enough.*'

'Henry, the Latimers seem to me to be, almost carrying around a sack full of guilt, where Daniel is concerned.'

'Yes...and that's tough for them to deal with. It can come from many sources...maybe from their own childhood baggage that they're carrying around in their adult lives. They end up transferring the effects onto their own children. A vicious circle, in a way, but we must acknowledge and remember that there is no absence of love in that family.'

Cartner drummed his fingers on the top of the file.

'John. Imaginary friends. Pretty commonplace in our line of business, eh?'

Stockley nodded.

'I told the Latimers to relax, not to worry. I told them, not exactly in these words, that imaginary, invisible friends are simply a manifestation of the way that children dream their dreams, build their aspirations, discover their wishes and desires....express their feelings....in a safe, private world of their own. In the same way that children regard cuddly toys, for example, as real live creatures. Children breathe life into them, so that they can cope with their journey of.....discovery.....of growing. A friend along the way.'

Henry drummed his fingers on the top of the file, then eased his large frame out of his chair and moved towards the window, where he prized apart a couple of the narrow dusty strips of the blind.

'Weather's getting distinctly cooler. Goodbye Summer' he remarked.

Stockley waited, as Henry drew on a length of cord to raise the blind, to allow the thin, watery light to flood into the office.

Henry resumed his seat 'Did you ever have one, John?'

'Have what?'

'An imaginary friend. When you were young?'

'No.'

'Why do you think that was the case?'

Stockley breathed in, heavily, 'Well I...we...had a pretty normal family, I suppose. As things went, a pretty happy gang. My brother and sister, growing up on a council estate in Redcar with our parents. Typical Teesside family. No real issues or problems to speak of. Plenty of pals. School friends. Still see a lot of them. I was never lonely. There was a house full most of the time: friends, neighbours, family and my mates. I suppose I never felt the need for another one. An imaginary one. Never happened.'

Henry smiled 'Of course you didn't. Don't you see? Children grow out of these things, usually because they have a family around them, an extended group of people who can show them that there is no need to escape to some make believe world. In your case, you could express yourself, discover yourself, grow up, in the safe haven of your family. You had no need of another world.'

He continued 'You didn't need another friend....Don't you see? In the vast majority of these cases, the imaginary friend is ..well...*invited*... welcomed even. The imaginary friend is created in the child's mind to become a support, a comfort, someone who will listen, someone to fill a gap

111

in a lonely life, or a confused life. When the problems disappear, the friend often disappears.'

'And in Daniel's case?'

Henry gazed across at the bookcase for a few moments, removed his handkerchief and blew his nose.

'In Daniel's case.....in Daniel's case, I don't see the invitation. Do you? There is no obvious evidence, it seems to me, that this boy had been anything other than a much loved, pretty normal, happy little boy. Just as you were in your family. It's as if this imaginary friend invited himself.'

Stockley could no longer guess where the conversation might take them and felt strangely uncomfortable, wrong footed by a sudden change of mood which had invaded the familiarity of the office. The smells and sounds of Henry Cartner's office, his spectacles, his handkerchiefs, his heavy jackets, his arm waving had always been fixed points of certainty. Not today. Today, the old boy seemed ill at ease with himself, a little bewildered, even confused at times. Stockley preferred the familiar.

'But what does that tell us about the drawing, Henry? I don't get it. You're surely not suggesting that, somehow, Daniel acquires special skills from his imaginary pal.'

Cartner allowed himself a broad smile 'No....I don't know. I simply don't know, but it seems to me that when Daniel's accident happened on that day, on the school field trip, it's as if this friend was waiting, waiting for...the chance.'

Stockley laughed quietly 'Almost like waiting for a gap in the market for mixed up kids?'

They both chuckled and Henry stood up, 'Almost...except that Daniel didn't display any signs of loneliness, or confusion. Still doesn't, in fact. Seems well adjusted, sure of his place in the world. Secure. No, John, this imaginary friend has invited himself in...'

From her small office adjacent to the main entrance lobby, Barbara could see the car pulling up outside and a familiar figure stepping out into the cool morning air. Claire Sissons opened the boot of her Renault Clio and retrieved her black carry case containing a laptop, some notes and a file of papers; the same carry case her parents had bought her, a few years ago, on the day of her graduation.

Barbara checked her diary, placed a pen in the top pocket of her uniform, and listened for the sound of the door buzzer; still waiting, holding back until one of the staff had released the security switch, and until the visitors book had been signed, and the antiseptic hand cleanser had been applied. Then she straightened her uniform and went out to greet her visitor from Social Services.

'Shall we go straight up to see him, Claire, or do you want a few minutes to go over his file?'

'If you have a spare, vacant bedroom, perhaps we could spend a couple of minutes going over things before the review. I have a number of calls, this morning.'

They used the lift to the first floor and walked cheerfully past the residents lounge towards the vacant bedroom.

'Where is he now? Does he know I'm coming?'

Barbara nodded without glancing into the room 'That's him in the armchair by the window. He spends more and more time in there these days, which is unusual. Thomas has never been a good mixer since he came to us, but lately he seems to want to be around the others. Doesn't say much, mind you, but it's probably doing him a bit of good to be out of his room. We like them to engage with each other, stops them brooding and keeps them going.'

They approached a small, quiet room which contained two armchairs, a low coffee table and bookcase full of worn paperbacks.

'Let's use this room Barbara, it's quiet and I'll only need a few moments.'

'To be honest, I can't remember the last time I saw any of the residents in this room. They're either in the lounge or in their own rooms.'

'Are we expecting anyone else?'

'What do you mean?'

'Relatives. Any of his family?'

'No.'

'So, what has happened with his previous assessments?'

'Well, Thomas gets his copy. That's it really. There's no family that I'm aware of. We have the name of a nephew somewhere. I think he was on his mother's side of the family, his mother was the sister of Thomas's wife. He lives in Nuneaton, I think. He came at the beginning to sort things out. His next of kin. He's there in the file as you'll see. He gets a copy of the assessment as well, and sorts out the financial side, I believe. Never visits though. Maybe once a year if that. No, he's on his own, I'm afraid. Thomas's wife died some time back and he'd been living on his own for few years before he came to us. Very private man, didn't want a great fuss. In fact, he could be a bit cantankerous at times....but then we're well used to that with old people. We could tell that he'd been a very intelligent man in his time. I suppose he's just grown old. I think he knew he was getting forgetful and wasn't really looking after himself properly. Comes to us all, like they say. Someone was telling me the other day that they heard he had been an engineer, you know, designing things. He would sit for ages reading and, sometimes, when he was in the mood, he would talk to one of the staff about computers and things like that. When he came to us, he was a little confused at times and his memory played tricks with him, but he was still very quick for a man of his age. He's not far off ninety now you know. Arrived with his books and things....and his computer. Sat for hours on his computer, in his room.'

Claire spread some papers on the coffee table.

'Does he still do that?'

'On his computer you mean? No. Not any more. I think it got a bit too much for him, maybe. He had it rigged up in his room, with a printer and everything so he could print things. One of the girls used to get her husband to bring in paper for him. We keep a float of money for each of the residents, to pay for the hairdresser, or newspapers. He used to dip into it to pay for his paper. Time was that he could manage things like that and there was no trouble with getting him to understand things, like money. But he's deteriorated lately and withdrawn. Like I said, we never see him on his computer now. Just sits quiet.'

'Does he watch the television, or listen to the radio?'

'Sometimes. If there's football on the TV. He listens to the matches on the radio as well, and follows the Boro. Sometimes we can get him to talk a little bit about the Boro.'

'Oh well, he'd be popular in our family. My Dad has a season ticket.'

Barbara frowned with concentration 'When the gentleman who had the room next door to Thomas, Mister Latimer his name was, lovely old gent... before he died...his young grandson used to come and they used to talk about the football. The staff used to talk about it. Made a real pal, he did, with that little lad.'

'You mean Thomas and Mister Latimer's grandson?'

'Oh yes. They would sit for ages. Sometimes in his room or, if the weather was nice, they'd sit in the garden.'

Claire glanced through the papers, then stared out of the window.

'Sometimes, with old people, they find a special affinity with children which they can't acquire from their contemporaries. We sometimes tend to assume that children and young people find old folk dull and boring, even a bit scary perhaps. The reality is often the opposite.'

'Funny really. They seemed good pals, and when I think about it now there seems to have been a big decline in Thomas since Mister Latimer passed away a few weeks ago.'

'Does he miss his neighbour? It would be a bit strange if he didn't.'

Barbara nodded 'We all miss Roy. But with Thomas, I think he'll miss the visits of that little lad and his family. That makes it harder for him.'

Claire sighed 'I can see that it would. Like a form of grief, really.'

Barbara looked at her watch and thrust her hand into her pocket to pull out a piece of note paper 'Mind you, there's this note. Got a call this morning. From Mrs Latimer, that's Roy's daughter in law. Daniel's mum. That's the young lad we've been talking about. She phoned to ask if it was alright to come on Sunday to take Thomas home for some Sunday lunch. I've heard they've got a lovely big house past Yarm way. Husband's an architect, you know.'

'This Sunday?'

Barbara nodded 'Yes. I wasn't sure at first, because Thomas hasn't been so lively, like I've said, and I thought it might upset and confuse him even more. But then, who am I to deny him? In the end, I think it might do him a bit of good, actually.'

Claire smiled 'I agree...does Thomas know?'

Barbara pushed the note back into her pocket and stood up 'We'll have to get on if you have other calls to make. I'll tell him now. I have a feeling it will cheer him up.'

19 The Cedars, Little Smeaton, early October 2005

Philip stared at the smiling face beneath the black mortar board, the slim fingers stretching out from the sleeves of the gown, clutching the rolled up graduation certificate; and barely recognised his father. The dining room had been rarely used since the house was built, Fiona and Richard preferring to eat around the large kitchen table, so that the spacious room at the front of the house had become strangely unfamiliar to their sons.

A large dresser contained a full dining set of Royal Doulton pieces, all shining white with their narrow, gold rims. Some had been removed by Fiona and placed carefully onto plain red table mats on the large, yew table in the centre of the room. Elsewhere on the dresser shelves were some tall, stemmed glasses, a couple of engraved goblets, two ginger bowls and a number of tiny thimbles. Three limited edition prints of local scenes had been hung in a row along the far wall. Against the opposite wall stood an occasional table on which a number of family photographs were arranged, most in plain silver frames containing sepia prints of long-gone relatives. Above them, on the wall, was the group of family photographs where Philip stood.

He winced at an early shot of himself with his brother, in identical tee shirts and shorts, hair neatly combed, facing the same way as if riding horseback on the same pony, set against a fierce blue studio background, identical smiles fixed to their glowing little faces. His parents in evening dress at a dinner dance, his grandfather Roy in a deckchair on the patio, Daniel in a plastic paddling pool on the lawn.

'Just put the knives and forks to one side, Phil, I'll sort them out in a minute.'

His shoulders slumped with a sigh as he ambled over to the huge bay window, the voice of his mother echoing across the quiet walls from the kitchen as he glanced over his shoulder to check that her list of instructions had been carried out. The sound of a car made him turn back to the window.

During the warm months of Summer, the red gravel drive had dried to a light salty pink colour, but the damp chill of early Autumn had returned it to a shade of dark plum. Now, it crackled with life as the family Peugeot appeared through the tall gates and slowly glided to a halt, adjacent to the front door.

His mother appeared at his shoulder, her hands encased in a pair of oven gloves.

'Thank you darling. They're here. Good.....come on....and smile!'

116

He remained at the window as she dashed out of the room, and felt the chill of a cool breeze through the front of the house as she opened the front door. He watched and waited as she ran out onto the drive, stooping and waving, her hands still wrapped in the oven gloves, and then Daniel jumping out of the Peugeot and scuttling around to his mother, then his thin little arms reaching inside the car. Richard emerged from the other side and stood next to Daniel as he fussed and fretted. The three of them were huddled together, obscuring his view, until, finally, Philip could make out a pair of sturdy, brown, brogue shoes gingerly planting themselves on the deep plum gravel, and Thomas's head bent low as he was hoisted to his feet. The old man was smiling as Daniel tugged at his hand, and then he noticed his brother climb back inside the car to retrieve a plastic shopping bag from the rear seat.

Their voices were getting louder now as they entered the house, so he went into the hall and stood to one side as they shuffled inside.

'You remember Phil?' enquired Fiona.

Thomas wobbled a little and held up his right hand in greeting.

'Philip. Yes, of course I do. How is your team doing?'

Philip smiled and grunted a quiet response, 'Top.'

'Long way to go yet though. Only November. It's a long season, you know.'

Philip peered at the old man, 'October....it's October.'

Daniel took Thomas's hand 'Do you want to see my room. I could show you my things. My computer and everything. Do you want to?'

Fiona was beaming 'Give him a chance, darling. Here, let me take your coat. I think perhaps we should sit down for now. Lunch won't be long. Come on, let's sit in the conservatory.'

Thomas's shoes squeaked along the shiny floor as he followed her through to the kitchen, where he stopped to look around at the large wooden table, the pans boiling away on the hob, the extractor breathing in the steam; then on to the conservatory. Richard beckoned him to settle on to a broad wicker chair while Fiona poured orange juice into tall, dark blue glasses before retiring to the kitchen.

The old man pointed to Daniel's hands 'Would you mind passing me that bag?'

Richard's eyebrows rose in slight surprise at the nimble manner in which Thomas untied his shoe laces, removed his brogues and put on his slippers.

'Don't wear shoes much these days,' he whispered, before taking a sip of orange juice. 'Thank you, this is nice. Very nice.' He took a longer sip, placed the glass down on the low table by his side, and stood erect to survey the garden and the patio.

The lines on Thomas's face began to slacken and ease into a relaxed smile as his eyes darted around the garden furniture, the cold frames, the patio ornaments, down to the lawn, the high hedge and the trees in the far corner.

'Lovely....lovely garden.' His face was grinning now.

Suddenly, his head turned slightly while his eyes never strayed from a mature apple tree, against which a ladder was leaning.

'Eva!' he exclaimed, a tremble of excitement catching his throat, 'Come and look at this.....lovely.'

Philip glanced at Daniel whose eyes were fixed on one of the large ceramic tiles which decorated the conservatory floor, then at his father who removed a large Sunday newspaper from one of the wicker chairs, scratched his nose and sat down. He waited for one of them to speak, feeling warm and clumsy as he edged closer to the old man's side.

Richard whispered desperately 'Phil...' but it was Thomas's voice which pierced the moment,

'My brother used to enjoy football a lot, just like you,' as his hand gently brushed the boy's hair.

They settled back into the wicker chairs and sipped from the blue glasses until Fiona ushered them through to the dining room where Thomas was offered a seat at the head of the table.

'Shall I just serve it onto your plate, Thomas? Would that be easier? Yes, I think so. Probably, yes? Don't worry if you can't manage everything. I hope you like roast beef and Yorkshire. As I said, don't worry if you can't eat it all. The boys have good appetites, don't they Richard?'

'What's this?' enquired Philip, his fork probing at a small jar in the centre of the table.

'Horseradish,' said Richard.

Thomas secured his napkin firmly into the neck of his cardigan,

'This looks very nice. Thank you. My appetite is not what it used to be, but I'll try to do justice. To tell the truth, the meals are quite good at Airdale. This is lovely. Eva is a good cook. Yes, you certainly have a fine house. Lovely.'

'Thank you. We love it,' smiled Fiona.

118

He turned to Richard, 'I expect you spent many hours working out the calculations for the open hall; all that space around the staircase, the load bearing walls above the landing, quite a challenge.'

Richard set down his knife and fork and quickly wiped his lips with his napkin.

'Highways man myself,' the old man continued, 'roads and bridges. Not the same level of artistry, I'm afraid. But buildings, architecture, that's a lovely thing. To be an architect. I know your father was proud. Quite rightly so.'

'Thank you....yes. Well, it was...as you say. Quite a challenge,' Richard took a sip of water.

'Don't mind me, Richard. I know I'm an old duffer but I'm not totally gaga. Not quite, yet. Some things you never forget. Engineering, architecture, things like that. They're in the blood. Like nature, trees. If your mind works that way, then these things stick with you...even if other things fly away.'

Richard laughed gently and they relaxed into the rest of the meal.

As Fiona poured coffee into the white Royal Doulton cups, Daniel slid away from his chair,

'Would you like to see my room now?'

'Let Thomas sit for a while to let his meal settle. You've done really well, Thomas, cleared your plate....I'm so glad you enjoyed it.'

'Lovely, thank you,' replied the old man.

Daniel said 'I'll just go upstairs then. You can come up when you're ready.'

'If I can manage all those stairs after all that food. Not used to stairs these days, living at Airdale. You get a bit stiff. But I'll be up in a minute. Your Dad will give me a hand, I'm sure.'

Daniel grinned and skipped out of the room, followed by his brother.

Thomas gently fingered his coffee cup and sighed, 'He's a fine little lad. You have two fine boys. Fine boys.'

Fiona rose from the table and began to clear away some dishes

'We've been so lucky, Richard and I. We know we have a lot to be thankful for.'

She stacked the dishes and began on the cutlery. 'Look, you two take your time. Relax for a few minutes, Thomas. I know Daniel has been so excited about you coming today, but kids can be tiring. You just say when you're ready to go up to see him. Any more coffee?'

119

When Thomas smiled and held up his hands, Fiona took it as a signal to leave the two men alone.

Richard shuffled awkwardly in his seat and cleared his throat 'Do you have any family?' Immediately, he regretted the question as a frown etched itself on the old man's face.

'We would have enjoyed children, Eva and I. But it didn't happen. The years went by and it just didn't happen. In the end, you adjust. You get used to life without them. Just the two of you. Then.....one day.....there's just one of you.. Just memories.'

The smile returned to his face 'Now, why don't you show me this marvellous staircase and young Daniel's room ?'

Richard drew back his chair and placed a hand, gently, under Thomas's elbow.

'Old bones, I'll be fine once I get moving. Just takes me a few moments to get going. Bloody nuisance.'

Richard stood directly behind Thomas at the bottom of the staircase and pointed out various features, before they began a nervous ascent, one step at a time, towards the landing, stopping once or twice for a breather. He was surprised at the old man's tenacity and determination.

'Well done,' he whispered, as they stood on the landing and leaned against the banister rail.

Thomas soon recovered 'Maple. You've done the doors in maple. Very good. That's beautiful.'

'Thank you.'

The old man winked 'Lead on.'

Thomas followed the direction of Richard's pointing arm, glancing at each of the doors in turn until he came to the one with the white ceramic name plate, which he stroked lightly with the tip of his right forefinger. The door was slightly ajar, so he gently pushed it open and walked inside.

'You're a lucky lad, you are. When I was a boy, I had to share with my brother.'

Daniel leapt to his feet, his face shining with eager delight as the old man surveyed the room, taking in the bright curtains, the dim light filtering through from the garden, the wall posters, the books and bags arranged next to the desk.

'Look, this is my computer. This is where I sit to do my work and all that stuff. I can do quite a lot with it. Like yours where you live. Do you want to try it?'

Thomas chuckled and walked towards the window.

'No thanks. It looks a good one, but I think I'd like to get away from computers today. Don't you get tired of them, sometimes?'

Daniel smiled and shook his head, 'No.'

Thomas peered out of the window.

'Lots of trees. Look at them. Lovely.'

Richard joined him at the window.

'Dan had to do a nature project for school. Seemed to enjoy doing that. In fact, he has quite a collection of things, you know, leaves and things. Did a good job, didn't you son?'

Daniel was silent.

'Pal of mine likes to collect birds eggs and things. Always up trees,' said Thomas.

Daniel looked at his father, his mouth slightly open then shutting as his father aimed a wink at him.

The old man went on 'Any greenfinches?'

Daniel went to Thomas's side and took his hand 'Don't think so.' He felt the warmth of the old man's hand wrap around his own and was strangely comforted by it, happy to stand and gaze out of the window into the grey skies. He jumped as his father's hand reached behind and tapped him on the shoulder. When he turned, Richard nodded down at the large red and black folder in the far corner of the bedroom, and he slipped his hand from Thomas's to retrieve it.

'Come and have a look at his drawings. I think you'll like these,' said Richard as he eased Thomas back into the room where Daniel had unfastened the folder and removed some pencil drawings and crayon sketches, spreading them carelessly on the bed.

'Hmm....yes. Yes,' the old man seemed to be fumbling for words as he picked each drawing up, examined it for a few seconds, and returned it to the bed. Then he picked up the folder itself and admired it, and felt inside it to retrieve some more of the contents. When he had finished he looked at Daniel.

'They are good. They are good. You should keep it up, son. I remember when you brought one of your drawings to show me, before, at Airdale, the one you brought to show your Granddad, and you brought it into my room. The drawing of the building, the tall thin building. Beautiful drawing. Do you remember?'

Daniel nodded.

Thomas nodded back, 'It was very good. I remember it.' His eyes met Richard's,

'Your wife must be waiting for some help.'

Richard looked blank 'Sorry.....my wife?'

'With all that washing up, in the kitchen.'

'Oh. I see.....well, yes. We have a dishwasher.....'

Thomas returned the blank stare.

'But your right. Fi could do with a hand.'

The old man rested his hand on Daniel's shoulder 'I'd like to look at these again. I think I've left my glasses in the bag I brought my slippers in. Could you get them for me, but first make sure you give your Mum a hand. Yes?'

When Daniel had left the room, Thomas turned to Richard.

'Now sir.....let us speak. Hmmmm? I'm going a bit potty. But I'm not completely ga-ga yet. That drawing. The one I was talking about just now. You still have the photograph I sent to you?...Yes?'

Richard began to speak but Thomas interrupted,

'You must have been a bit....surprised with that. I'm sorry, very sorry if that caused you alarm, it wasn't what I meant to do, but I had to do something. When I first saw Daniel's drawing I thought I must have already gone round the bend. Kept looking at my photograph, taking out of my drawer, putting it back again. Remembering the drawing. Trying to keep calm. Feeling lonely and confused like the sad old man that I am. It was as though everything was blurring together in one big heap in my mind. All mixed up together. Every detail in Daniel's drawing was the same, every window, the roof, everything, just the same. Couldn't just ignore it. You do see that? That's what this is about, yes? I'm not completely bloody daft, Richard. You've been most kind. All of you. Lovely. Really lovely. But I expect you want to know about the photograph, the drawing and all of that. Make some sense of it all? From a daft old man.'

'You're not daft, Thomas. Certainly not daft.'

'Not yet....but it won't be long now.' He sighed. 'The days are drawing in, every day gets harder to just....I don't know...focus. Can't seem to focus. Some days are better than others. This is a good day, and I want to thank you and I want to help you. Let me help you while I can. Let me. I want to. And I think you want me to, don't you?'

Richard's head bent forward and he hugged himself.

Thomas continued 'I know that building. The one in the drawing. You know that.... I know it. Just as in the drawing. The photograph I sent you. I can show you where it is......if you like. Show you....if you want?'

Richard seemed on the verge of collapsing into himself, his face grey with anguish as he felt the warmth of the old man's hands resting on his shoulders, his breath inches away from his cheek.

'I know you are so worried about the boy, but let me help.'

Richard breathed in deeply, and straightened up as if in defiance of the onset of tears, his jaw tight, his eyes focussed on a distant point somewhere along the line of maple doors. He nodded his head.

'Yes. Yes. Let's do that, Thomas. Show me.'

Thomas let his arms slowly drop from the younger man's shoulders.

'Are you up for it? Today? This afternoon?'

Thomas looked surprised ' Don't understand these new bloody expressions. Up for it. You mean what exactly?'

Richard smiled 'This afternoon, while it's quite fine and dry, you me and Daniel. We could go for a drive to this place. You could show us. We could do it. What do you think?' His eyes blazed with pleading, animated to a degree that Thomas had not thought possible in the man.

Thomas slowly turned his back on him and began the return journey along the landing towards the summit of the staircase.

'I'm up for it,' he said.

The last time she had sat in this rather uncomfortable chair, alone in Henry Cartner's office, bright sunlight had dazzled her eyes and exposed a thin layer of grey dust on the window blinds. Fiona had not previously experienced this drab little room as it now was, flooded in white illumination from the narrow strip lights on the ceiling. She fidgeted with her watch for a few moments, the one that Richard had brought back from a business trip to Singapore, three years ago, to say thanks for her support when Roy had had to be persuaded to go into the Care Home at Airdale. Those were the days when she had the boys at her word, and could walk them both into the village and back and know that they would not run off; when she could bundle them in the car and know that they would both be eager and excited just to be going for a ride together; when she could reassure them with a cuddle and not have to rely on her husband's support.

Her fingers reached down to brush her skirt and then played with the handle of the large shopping bag which was resting against her legs. She moved the bag to one side and propped it up against the legs of the chair as her eyes strayed over towards the row of thick, heavy books which lined the top shelf of the bookcase. They had probably remained undisturbed for months, perhaps years.

Fiona imagined what sort of a child Henry had been. A large, ungainly boy, she thought. Probably a little clumsy. Bright in his own way, studious, with a small circle of friends. Eager to please his parents and teachers. Maybe teased by other kids…but big enough to handle it somehow. Not into mischief very much, nor sports. No, Henry would not have been a footballer at school though he may have feigned interest in cricket and might have taken up fishing, although those large hands would have struggled with tying flies. More than likely, he joined the chess club. Passed his eleven plus, of course. Then, when he grew older…..

She fiddled with her watch again.

Folk clubs maybe. Yes, Henry may have been into that scene for a while. At Uni. In his Arran sweater and sporting a shaggy beard. But not for long. ……..

Still, what the heck. None of that mattered now. It was Thomas, the old man going ever so slowly downhill who had saved her life; saved it and cared for it, and returned it to her. Thomas who had found the key to unlock the demons in Daniel's head and set them free. Not Henry. Henry had been there throughout, at the end of a telephone, reachable through an appointment, waiting, here in this office, to listen. That's all he had done, good old Henry. Listened long and carefully. Giving words of comfort and support. For that alone, she would always think kindly of him. But it had been Thomas... She giggled to herself. Henry, Thomas. Such grand old names. Her mind raced back to the last time that she had pronounced those names aloud in the same breath, when she had read the stories of Thomas the Tank Engine to Daniel. When he was....what.....four....or five?

She was still smiling when Henry entered the room, bearing a tray with two multi coloured mugs, an orange teapot, white milk jug and a bright blue sugar bowl.

'Sorry about that. My secretary's on a course today and the other girl is on leave and...Sorry, I'll just put this down here, shall I?'

'My line I think...shall I be mother?'

Henry chortled quietly and nodded towards the shopping bag at Fiona's feet, 'Ah, doing some Christmas shopping. I'm afraid I'm terribly dysfunctional when it comes to shopping of any sort, I need organising I'm afraid and..'

'Not shopping, no. Some other things. Shall I pour?'

Henry sat back and watched her carefully pour from the teapot, finger nails gleaming, slender fingers gripping the handle so that the knuckles shone, white and almost translucent.

'I expect you are all looking forward to Christmas?'

'The boys haven't said much yet, but once the schools start to wind down for the end of term, the excitement will start.'

Henry nodded slowly and took a sip from one of the multi coloured mugs.

'How is Daniel doing at school? Are things still going well?'

Fiona placed her hands in her lap.

'Yes. Yes, he seems to have settled well. We're keeping a close eye of course but the Head is very pleased with the progress he's making. Much like his old self. We're very pleased.'

Henry gripped the mug in his large hands, the rim just a few inches away from his lips, so that the steam began to cloud his spectacles. He ignored it.

'Well, as you know, John and I have seen him on a number of occasions in the last six weeks and I have to say.....well.....we are very reassured by his progress. Quite remarkable progress. As you say, his school reports are most encouraging. What about general behaviour, in the home, with his pals, with Philip, with his father? Whenever we've seen him and spoken to the rest of you, the news has been good. Is this still the case?'

Fiona was beaming now 'I can't begin to tell you what a relief it is to hear the boys doing what they're supposed to do at their age, you know what I mean don't you? Playing, joshing each other, arguing, the way they used to, about boyish things.'

Henry placed the mug onto the tray 'And there's been no repeat of...no return of...'

For a second the smile became fixed, the mouth hardening almost in a reflex response to the question as Fiona shook her head 'No. None.'

'You must be very relieved.'

'Well, I recall that from the very start you have tried to reassure Richard and I that these things are often passing phases. That he would grow out of it. We're so grateful for what you have done here.'

Henry removed his spectacles and fixed his gaze at her.

'Mrs Latimer.....Fiona, I am, of course, very pleased with the way things have gone with your son. However, I have a confession to make, in the sense that....well...while the sessions we have had here have undoubtedly helped Daniel, and I trust all of you, to deal with his problem and to cope with it, in a supportive sense that is, well I...have to confess that, while it is perfectly true that most children who go through these phases in their life can just as easily come out of them....I confess....'

'That you really have no idea what was really going on with Daniel.'

Henry replaced his spectacles, 'I would like to understand more. I realise and appreciate your relief, which we all share, but I would like to understand more and...if you would mind, I wonder if you could, please, help me with this just a little longer. The catalyst, the trigger don't you see? I would very much like to know what happened to produce this transformation in your boy. I need to know what happened on that day, a couple of months ago. We touched on it in our previous sessions, but...'

Fiona sighed, the fingers of her right hand gently stroking her chin, 'We told you about the photograph, and Thomas, and the day he came to lunch.'

Henry nodded 'Please...could you explain it again. The detail, every detail. Then, I promise, we will draw a line under all of this and get on with our lives. Mmmm, what do you say? I would be most grateful.'

'After lunch we cleared up a few things. The day was quite bright, still, pleasant really and we all squashed into the car. Richard and I were in the front and the boys were sat on either side of Thomas. It felt very strange, the whole business of Thomas coming to lunch with us but I suppose, at that point, I was just relieved that it had all gone well and the old chap seemed to be enjoying himself. He and Daniel were quiet once we set off and it wasn't long before Phil started up, wanting Richard to put the car radio on so that he could listen to the football commentary. So that's what we did. Listened to the match as we drove towards Billingham along the A19, over the flyover past those ghastly chimneys and factories and the prison and turned off at Norton to back towards Billingham Bank and so on. It wasn't until then that Thomas chirped up. Good grief, he said, those white houses haven't changed much.

We drove on, up the bank, towards the old village part and turned left at the top, next to the pub. Thomas was more animated now, making the odd comment here and there. Lots of the old houses have gone. New bungalows. Daniel was quiet, and then....'

Henry remained motionless.

'Something made me turn around to look at Daniel. I didn't want to but I knew I had to because this was very near to where he had been so upset that day when I had taken him out to collect things for his nature project. He was pale and shrinking into Thomas's coat, gripping his hand tightly. It was all there, just the same: the old church, the funny gate thing, the lych gate, the church yard, the shops. Thomas suddenly called out. Stop. Richard pulled the car into a little side road in front of the lych gate and we sat there for a few moments. The match commentary was still blaring out, I remember, and it seemed so out of place somehow but, I don't know, it was a also a comforter, a weird link to reality. One son absorbed in the reality of a football match while the other was so clearly trapped in a strange little world of his own, far removed from all of that. I didn't want to let go of reality and I remember thanking God for Phil. Isn't that scary, and terribly shameful?'

Henry smiled and shook his head.

'There was no one about in the churchyard or the path leading up to the old church, Saint Cuthbert's, but a few people were milling about the little shops around the green, and there were some cars parked up near the row of cottages close to the church hall. Thomas was pointing at a flat area of grass, a sort of triangular shape, perfectly flat, which separated the main road through the village from the church, like a bit of a roundabout set back from the road. He said that this was where the building had stood. On that spot. The building in the old photograph. The same spot that Daniel had shrunk away from in frightened tears on that awful bloody morning in Summer. I could see that Daniel was still clinging to Thomas, but I couldn't bring myself to speak, for fear of setting him off again. We just, sort of, sat in frozen silence for a few seconds.'

Fiona stopped and took a sip of tea. Henry noticed that the small beginnings of a smile had begun to spread on her lips, which had left their customary red stain on the rim of the mug.

'Half time. It was Phil who broke the mood. Half time, he said. I remember the feeling of relief, like a prompt, a reminder that we were still together, there was a bond between us and now this old man, Thomas, was a part of that bond. I wasn't going to allow anything or anybody to break it. Not a mood, not a feeling, no one. I remember that Richard was gripping the steering wheel of the car, staring ahead, so I tapped the back of his hand and told him to drive on.'

Henry leaned forward a little, 'How was Daniel, at this point?'

'Very quiet, and that was a relief really. I don't know what I'd imagined might happen, when we returned to the place by the old church, but there was no crying or yelling from him. Thomas was holding his hand, all the time. I don't know....'

'Go on....you don't know what?'

'Well....it was if, somehow, *they* had perhaps been expecting something to happen which didn't actually materialise. But that might be just a feeling. Who knows what was going on in their heads, at the time?'

'Hmmm. Thank you. Thank you for this. Please go on.'

'Well, we drove off through Billingham, past the shops and so on towards the Bottoms. Thomas was quiet again, just peering out at the houses and so on. We pulled in at the little gate off the dual carriageway where the recreation park, Billingham Beck, Bottoms, or whatever they call it now... ecology park...nature park...'

'I know what you mean.'

'There were one or two people about, enjoying the day, the weather had held and the light was only just starting to fade. A young couple were sitting on the wooden benches, while some other people were returning from a walk along the paths by the beck, coming towards the picnic area near where we were parked up, next to the wooden hut thing, the visitors centre. I remember thinking, this is really rather pleasant; I could understand why the school had wanted to bring Daniel and his chums on their nature trip. Richard got out of the car first and I watched as he paced a few yards and stretched out his arms, something I had not seen him do for ages. Funny how you remember little things like that, isn't it?'

Henry smiled, 'Would you like a refill? Some more tea?'

'Thanks. No. I'm fine.'

Fiona reached down and felt the handle of her shopping bag, as if to reassure herself that it was still there.

'Shall I move that somewhere for you? By my desk perhaps?'

'No...thank you, really. I'm fine.'

'As long as you're comfortable. I really do appreciate this. Thank you.'

'Daniel helped Thomas out of the car, I think he must have been a bit stiff, the old boy, but he seemed OK. Richard walked around to the back of the car and opened the boot, so that we could put on coats and wellies and so on, as you do...When we were ready, we started to walk towards the little path by the beck, Thomas and Daniel at the front, where we could keep an eye on them. Thomas had his arm around Daniel's shoulder and I remember that he held him close for a second then stopped and asked him, Where did you fall out of the tree? Show me. Daniel pointed to a place probably about thirty yards away. I'm not sure really, not much good at distances. At that moment, Phil gave me a nudge to let me know that he wasn't bothered about walking anywhere but he wanted to go back to the car to listen to the rest of the football match. Richard gave him the keys and off he went. Thomas was chuckling a little and gave Daniel's hair a quick rub. Come on. Take me to this tree of yours.'

Henry crossed his legs, 'Did you all go on?'

'No. We sort of took the hint, Richard and I, and stayed rooted to the spot while Daniel and Thomas went on ahead, on their own. I remember that I gave Daniel a car rug just in case they needed to sit down, with Thomas being a bit shaky on his feet. He rested his hand on Daniel's shoulder and off they went towards the tree, with Daniel leading the way, the car rug rolled up and wedged under his arm. I have to say, they looked a strange pair, the two of them, and we felt distinctly awkward hovering there, just watching them from a distance.'

'How did they seem to you, Fiona? Happy, sad, nervous?'

'No. None of those things really. In fact, it was all very...calm, orderly. They made their way to the spot by the tree, but we couldn't see their faces as they were walking away from us. Couldn't hear their voices either. If they had been talking, then it must have been in whispers because we couldn't hear them at all. When they reached the tree, of course, they were too far away for us to hear any chatter. I remember trying my best to look relaxed and casual, next to Richard. As if this was all very, nothing out of the ordinary. Stupid. It *was* normal to the few folks that were about; just an old man and a boy on a peaceful Sunday afternoon. Could have been his granddad. But to me it felt weird, strange, and a bit unreal. I don't know what was I was expecting to happen.'

'So, what *did* happen when they reached the tree?'

'Well, they looked around a bit, and then Daniel put his hands on the trunk as if to start climbing, but then stepped back and pointed upwards to the branches, obviously showing Thomas the branch that he'd managed to reach on the day of the accident. Thomas was nodding, his head cocked on one side as if listening intently, you know, the way that we grown ups do to show that they are giving the child their full attention. I looked rather sweet, to be honest. After a few moments, Daniel dropped the car rug onto the ground and began to spread it out, very carefully unfolding it so that it covered as much grass as possible, beneath the tree. Then, he took Thomas by the hand and helped him to crouch down on the rug. So very gently. They were chatting for a while, then we could make out that they were silent. For ages, it seemed to me. Then, I don't know when exactly, they were talking again. Differently now. Even from thirty yards, I could see that the conversation had changed. I remember looking sideways at Richard, but his expression was flat and a bit drained, and I knew that he was as uncomfortable as I was, because I felt him take my hand.'

'I'm sorry, I don't understand. What had changed? They were just chatting away under the tree weren't they?'

'Oh sure, they were talking. But now it was more animated…it was if… there was somebody else there. Another person, sat on that rug on the ground with them.'

The spectacles had been removed, once more, from Henry's nose.

'Are you sure, Fiona? Another person? How can that be? I don't understand?'

'It's hard to explain. We were just staring across at the two of them, but…it was as if there were three. Just the way they kept on moving their heads; their expressions; their faces; movement, nodding here and there and gesturing; all the things we do when we are talking in a little group; Thomas and Daniel were doing all those things. Talking away.'

'Were you afraid?'

'Not really, no. Not at that point anyway. They looked so natural. But then, they started to laugh, as if sharing a private joke with each other, and patting each other on the shoulder. That made me start to feel uneasy.'

'Why?'

'Because then, it really did seem as though there *were* three of them, even though we could only see Daniel and Thomas; it seemed for all the world that there were three of them under that tree. Weird or what? Then.

Then the laughter turned to tears and I really became quite agitated. A mother knows when her son is upset from a hundred yards away, never mind thirty, so I knew something was wrong and the feeling of wanting to run over to him was almost overwhelming. I think Richard must have sensed my alarm because I remember wincing as his fingers tightened their grip on my hand, holding me back.'

'Daniel was crying? What about the old man?'

Fiona nodded, 'I'm sure he must have been. He kept cradling his forehead, shielding his eyes, and his shoulders were all scrunched up. It's more difficult to tell with old people, and folk that you don't really know that well, but yes, I would have to say that Thomas was crying as well. I'm sure he was.'

'Did you go over to them?'

'No. We just stood there and watched, and waited. One second they were crying, then they would be smiling and laughing, and hugging each other; and they went on that way for ages until, finally, both of them were quiet and still, motionless. Richard suggested that we walk over to them but, the second that we started to move, I noticed that Daniel had started to clamber to his feet, so I pulled Richard back, and we resumed our position. Daniel was crouching down to allow Thomas to lean on his shoulders to haul himself up. When the pair of them had scrambled to their feet, I noticed that the old man stood to one side, as if under instruction from Daniel while he picked up the car rug, shook it vigorously, and began to fold it into a roll. Daniel seemed very much in charge of the situation, as though he'd assumed control. I don't know why but that made me laugh a little.'

'Did the two of them come straight back over to where you and your husband were standing?'

'Not straight away, no. There were a few moments of silence again as Thomas seemed to steady and compose himself. I didn't think he was ill or anything like that but he rested his hand again on Daniel's shoulder before they started to walk towards us. It was then that I began to feel...to notice...'

Henry leaned forward.

'It was as if their faces had somehow, changed, altered. No. That's not what I meant to say. This is so hard to describe. Just give me a second or two......not their faces exactly.'

'You mean their expressions? The look on their faces, perhaps?'

'The look on their faces. Yes. On Daniel, and on Thomas. Both the same. The same look.'

'I'm really sorry Fiona. You'll have to explain.'

'Well. They both looked *alive*. Both of them. So *alive*. There was a look in their eyes as they approached, I could make it out from quite a distance but once they were within a few yards it was so clear and sharp. Identical brightness, shining. How can I explain? Imagine Imagine the joy in the eyes of a child when it opens a longed for Christmas gift; that was how it seemed. Oh, I could see for myself the tear stains on Daniel's cheeks; like I said, a mother always know when her child's been crying , but they were as nothing compared to the bright glowing in his eyes.'

'What did they say? Anything? Were they excited, happy, sad?'

'They were calm, both of them, calm. When they were getting close to us, Daniel ran to his father and hugged him. The car rug dropped to the ground and Thomas started to bend down to try to retrieve it but he couldn't quite manage it, so I reached down to give him a hand. Daniel came to me then and we held each other for a few moments, before Thomas spoke. He told me that I was going to be fine now. That Daniel was going to be fine. He kept on repeating it.'

Henry withdrew the handkerchief from the breast pocket of his jacket and held it for a few seconds before removing his spectacles and giving them a wipe.

'And what was that? Nothing more was said or done? You went home?'

To be honest, the rest of it is more of a blur, now. I remember us being in the car. The football was finishing on the radio. Funny that. The whole episode had felt like a funny sort of dream that had lasted for hours, and yet it could only have been for a short while, half an hour or so, maybe a little more. The football commentary hadn't even finished. How strange. Phil had been sitting there, in the car, as if nothing much had been going on and yet the rest of us had been playing out this curious sort of...I don't know... weird little drama. And there was singing. We were singing in the car, on the way home. I can't even remember what it was. Something the boys knew from school. Probably a bit rude, but I didn't care, not a bit. I just knew that we were back, together, all of us.'

'What about Thomas? How was he?'

'He seemed happy and content, but a little tired. Come to think of it, he must have been exhausted. Poor old chap had had more exercise in a single day than he'd had for many a month, I expect. Richard dropped off the boys and I, back home at the Cedars; we gave Thomas a quick hug and then Richard took him back to Airdale Lodge.'

'And was everything alright with Thomas, did Richard say? Did you husband mention anything about the journey back to Airdale? I know it might seem strange to be dwelling on all of this detail, but it really does help me to understand a little better about Daniel, about his relationships. You've been so helpful, I really do appreciate this. Really, I do.'

'Well, he took quite a bit longer than I had expected to get back from the Care Home and at one point I remember being a little concerned. Not so much about Richard, but a little anxious about Thomas, in case we'd exhausted him.

I heard the car pull up in the drive and I expected him to come straight into the kitchen to see how the boys were, grab a cup of tea, or something. But he didn't. I heard the car door go, and then he opened the front door and went straight upstairs. That seemed strange but I didn't give it too much thought, I was still on a bit of a high. It was good few minutes before Richard appeared downstairs.'

'Something was up?' Henry's voice was little more than a whisper.

'Well no, not really, he seemed quite relaxed and content, as we all were, of course. Still, I could see that he was preoccupied with something. He told me that Thomas had seemed very tired but otherwise fine, having enjoyed the day with us, and had asked that his thanks be passed on, for lunch and everything else.

Then, Richard mentioned that he had some things to do, papers that he had to finish in time for a meeting with some clients in the morning, things that he had to read and prepare. I have to admit I was bit miffed because I'd envisaged a quiet evening at home, all four of us together. But I wasn't going to allow anything to prick my bubble, so I just kissed him and he held me for a few moments…and off he went, while I prepared some sandwiches and crisps for me and the boys. Just the three of us settle down to watch some telly.'

'You must have felt very relieved, I imagine.'

'Very happy and relieved, yes. I can't remember what we watched that evening. To be honest, it was enough just to have my boys with me, together, in that way. And I remember feeling tired. At some point much later, Phil and Dan went off to their rooms and I popped up soon after to look in on them and make sure that they were getting ready for bed. The way they used to when they were much smaller. When I got back to the kitchen, I remember making myself a hot milk drink in the microwave and deciding that I would turn in for an early night. Then, I heard Richard coming downstairs.'

Henry smiled. 'So, he'd been working away all evening? It's a hard life running your own business, I suppose.'

As he waited for any form of small response, Fiona ran her left hand through her hair, and he realised that of all her little gestures and hand movements, this one had , up to this moment, gone unnoticed.

'He was holding some things in his hands, in a very odd sort of way, almost as if they hot and straight from the oven, beginning to scald. When I looked a little closer, I could see that there was a newspaper and a file of papers. It just seemed a little odd to me but I assumed that they were to do with the business, so I scolded him a little about working until late and neglecting me and the boys…but not in a nasty way…just joshing a little, teasing. He put the things down on the kitchen table and I asked him how Thomas had been when he took him back to Airdale. There was a bit of a silence and for just a second I remember feeling a tightness in my throat, especially when he put his hands on my shoulders and told me to sit down next to him, because he wanted to tell me something important. So I did.'

'Was he upset? Did he seem distressed?'

'No, I wouldn't say distressed exactly, but clearly this was something that couldn't wait. He began by telling me that Thomas had seemed very relaxed and content in the car, and when they had pulled up at the Care Home, he was grateful that Richard had offered to see him to his room to make sure that he was OK. Everything was fine, and the staff had been very nice, welcoming him back and making a bit of a fuss.

Once inside Thomas's bedroom, he had seemed a little more agitated and had made straight to his little desk drawer, telling Richard that he had some things which he had wanted to give to him, for all of us really, as a way of saying thanks, showing his appreciation, and so on. I think Richard was very embarrassed but didn't want to seem ungracious, so he accepted them with good grace and came away. Anyway, when he returned home he took them straight upstairs. That was why he hadn't come straight into the kitchen you see, because he simply couldn't resist opening the *gifts* to see what they were. Like a big kid, really.'

'Quite,' grinned Henry.

'Naturally, I asked him what they were, and could I please see them, and he simply waved his arm over the kitchen table and nodded at the paper and the file. When I began to examine them, I could see that the newspaper was old and faded and rolled up as if to contain something, like a little package. I reached out for it, but Richard quickly intercepted.

'Fee,' he said, I'd leave it until the morning if I was you, once you've opened it up and started to read this…and he tapped the file…you won't want to stop.'

'How odd. Did you do as he suggested?'

'I'll admit I was intrigued but I took his advice. We both had a hot milk drink and I remember we put a drop of brandy in it, and that was that for the night. Next morning, when everyone was up and about their business, I took the

file and the old newspaper into the conservatory and began to read. Richard was bang on. I didn't stop until I'd read every last page. Thomas's gift. More like a legacy, really.'

Henry gave a loud sigh.

'Fiona, I really have no right to ask you what I'm about to request, but…'

'I know. You want the details.'

Henry nodded gravely and removed his spectacles as Fiona reached down into her shopping bag.

'I come bearing gifts. Thomas's gifts.'

Rising to her feet, she carefully placed in Henry's lap a hard back file with a yellow cover, and a rolled up faded newspaper.

'Merry Christmas, Henry.'

He placed the newspaper on the carpet and flipped over the hard yellow cover of the file, and managed to scan the first few words, *'My father's temper was like the wind'* before Fiona had reached the door.

'Everything you need to know is in there. It will help you understand,' she said. 'Oh and one more thing…something I wanted to ask you about childhood. Or rather your childhood, when you were a boy. Did you have a favourite hobby, you know…music? Bird watching perhaps?...anything like that?'

Henry stood with the yellow file in his large hands, and smiled.

'Rugby. I'm afraid it was an obsession.'

He could still hear her laughter as she departed down the corridor towards the reception area and, when he was certain that she would not be returning, he placed the file on his desk and retrieved the faded newspaper from the carpet. He placed it alongside the yellow file, as though he was about to unroll a treasure map, and his fingers felt a hard, circular object. Henry paused and began to unwrap he paper until an old tobacco tin emerged from its wrapping. It opened easily to reveal a bright shining pebble, a tiny glass marble and a small horses head carved in inky black jet.

He shifted his weight and shuffled around to the other side of his desk, then sagged into his chair. Henry stared at the telephone for a few moments but found himself resisting the temptation to ring John Stockley, and instead flicked over the pages of the yellow file to the last few passages.

EPILOGUE

'...it was the last time that I ever saw Jesse alive. The warm sun was darting bright rays through a curiously regular hole in the window, sending dancing patterns of light across the floor of that strange little room where he lay with a terrible, terrible look of sadness in his fading eyes. Blood came in a straight line, from his hand, along his arm.

'Go on!'
That's what he said. The last words I heard him say.
'Go on!'

Running, breathing hard, running, our feet hard, hard, hard, on the path, down the lane.
Bill and me.
Pounding, pounding to the Bottoms; a pain in my side where the tin rattled away in a steady rhythm, tight, locked inside my pocket.

Pah! I've been running ever since that day.

Until now.

Now, these bloody old legs of mine have slowed down. I can feel them... I can feel them slowing down. It doesn't hurt any more. All that running.
Moving about, dodging this and that, all of the obstacles in the way, missing them, going round them, under them. Running.

Running is a lonely business.

You can feel yourself breathing everywhere. Hear every breath. So loud.

Bloody hell it's been lonely running on my own. When I started, there was Bill on my side but I soon lost him along the way. Never the same after Jesse. Never could be. When I started running that day, running, running, running, from the Pinnacle, I wasn't just leaving Jesse behind. I was leaving it all, Bill, Joe, the others...I was leaving me behind. Where did they all go?
Bloody lonely without them.

Just a line of blood from his arm, flowing out onto the floor, and bits of broken pipe.

So they thought it was from the stranger; the one with half his face gone; the one who'd been seen hanging around our village for weeks until he disappeared as quickly as he'd arrived; the one the police never traced, all those years ago. For months there were stories and rumours; words spoken in huddled corners and whispered conversations, sightings in some far off place: he'd gone to Scotland, he'd drowned off the Northumberland coast. Sometimes I've dreamed he never even existed, but I had my little reminders, they never left me. Now even they've gone. To Daniel and his family. Thank the Lord.

Don't need reminders any more. Not now.

We moved a year later, to Middlesbrough, and my Dad got himself a job at the steel works.

Bloody lonely.

Our Bill went to work with our Dad and I kept on running. Away from the trees and becks and birds nests and into books and desks and chalk filled rooms and pens and pencils.

Running.

Into more books, harder books, bigger rooms, bigger people, along corridors, Constantine College, drawing boards.

Running to night class. To qualifications.

Further away from that bright light, the one that shone so fiercely from those cerulean blue eyes and still shines, somewhere, even now. Running away from it until it was just a glimmer, flickering away, fading...and leaving me lonely beyond pain until the only thing left was numbness; a dull numbness; a paid up, safe, respectable, professionally qualified numbness.

It was even lonely when Eva came along, but at least she managed to slow me down a bit. Just a bit. But even she didn't stop me altogether. Nobody could. Ever. Until now.

Until Daniel Latimer.

I knew straight away that he wasn't lonely, even though he was giving his folks such grief. I knew that kid wasn't lonely, not like I'd been all these bloody years. They thought he was sad and lonely, that kid. Sad and lonely? Never.

Then it was there you see, in that drawing, it was there again. The Pinnacle. He was there, we were there.
Oh, I know what you're thinking, but he was there. I could feel it there. The energy, the freedom, the trees and bushes, the trees and birds nests. I was there again. Under that tree on that perfect Sunday afternoon, he was definitely there, laughing, crying, I could feel his laughter, we could feel his tears.

And he said it was all right. It was done, finished. He was laughing with us.

Forgiven don't you see? You get it, don't you? It was all bloody right! No need to run any more!

Look at me now. Now you can see how I live in my twilight years, can't you?

No more running.

Ashgrove Education

We welcome synopses or ideas for books on educational subjects.

Our intention is to build a body of work that will actually make a difference within this important field.

Your submission may be within any field of education, including textbooks for the primary, secondary and tertiary levels.

We are not prescriptive about length or form but we ask you to remember that the length and form must be appropriate to the age and interests of the end users, whether youngsters or adults.

Texts suitable for teachers in training are also welcome. Or for teachers already qualified who may be seeking fresh ideas and texts that have common sense allied to vitality.

Send an outline of your idea as an email attachment to info@ashgrovehousepublishing.com.

Please insert EDUCATION in the subject box.

Ashgrove Crime

Ashgrove Crime invites authors to offer crime novels written according to the following guidelines:

- 30 000 to 40, 000 words.
- The story may be set in any part of the world.
- The story is told in the first or third person.
- The main plot tells how the protagonist, the hero, fights against the forces of evil within a particular society.
- Avoid sub-plots.
- Have a linear narrative – avoid flashbacks unless they are absolutely necessary.
- Build tensions – the forces or circumstances that prevent the hero achieving a quick resolution
- Achieve a satisfactory conclusion where the hero finally triumphs.

Be realistic. Set the story in a particular milieu. Contemporary settings are usually best.

Think Dashiell Hammett, James M. Cain, Raymond Chandler, the Black Mask authors, Hank Jansen, Mickey Spillane, Robert B. Parker – or any other successful crime writer of the past or present. But be sure the style and the story are your own. Scenes of violence are acceptable if within the plot and/or the characters. The same with scenes of graphic sex. Think carefully before these are added to your story.

Ashgrove Romance

Ashgrove Romance would like to invite authors to offer romance novels written according to the following guidelines:

- 30 000 to 40, 000 words.
- Think Harlequin/Mills & Boon.
- The story may be set in any part of the world.
- The story is told from the main female character's perspective.
- The story is told in the first or third person.

The **heroine** may be from any national or ethnic background; should experience personal growth and self-discovery; realise her own worth and inner strengths.

The **hero** is strong and may be successful in his chosen field. Is attractive to women.

The plot

- The main plot-line revolves around the heroine & hero's struggle to build a romantic relationship.
- outside forces (at work or in their communities) try to keep them apart.

Age groups: from teenagers to 65+, mainly but not entirely female.